I0418837

Leaves from Kashmir

Saba Shafi

Woven Words Publishers OPC Pvt. Ltd.

Registered Office:

Vill: Raipur, P.O: Raipur Paschimbar,

Dist: Purba Midnapore, Pin: 721401,

West Bengal, India.

www.wovenwordspublishers.in

Email: editor@wovenwordspublishers.in

Published by Woven Words Publishers OPC Pvt. Ltd., 2018

First published by Patridge India, 2017

Copyright© Saba Shafi, 2018

NOVELLA

ISBN 13: 978-93-86897-26-8

ISBN 10: 9386897261

Price: $15

This book is a work of fiction. All names, characters, places, addresses and incidents are fictitious and product of the author's imagination. Any resemblance with any events, locales, persons-living or dead, is purely coincidental.

The author asserts the moral right to be identified as the author of this work.

All rights reserved. This book is sold to the condition that it shall not, by way of trade or otherwise, be lent, resold, hired out, or otherwise circulated without the publisher's prior consent in any form of binding or cover other than that in which it is published and without a similar condition, including this condition, being imposed on the subsequent purchaser.

Printed and bound in India

For Kashmir, my home, my heart

The soul is a stranger

trying to find a home

somewhere that is not a where

         - ***Rumi***

Contents

.

Prologue
Chapter 1
Chapter 2
Chapter 3
Chapter 4
Chapter 5
Epilogue

Acknowledgements

Kun Fayakun!

Be, and it is!

'When He decrees a thing, He says to it "Be!" And it is.'

Surah Baqarah, The Holy Quran (2.117).

My humble pen can write simple stories, but it cannot find enough words to pen down the Glory of The Master Storyteller, The Light Manifest, The Creator and His Creation. So, I simply bow my head.

Manan, my husband, my mirror, my love (and hate!), who kept embracing the ugly in me, until he transformed it into something beautiful: who kept picking and joining, as I kept throwing and breaking. Thank you for being steadfast, for pushing me to write this, for making it a reality. Thank you for being.

How this story got written by me, through me, is nothing short of a miracle. One phone call, one reality check, one shaking up of the soul is all that was needed to help me string the scattered beads of pearl lying before my eyes all along and make a necklace that would adorn my neck and those that choose to wear it. Kareena, thank you for being the calming force in my life, for assuring me that no matter what the world thought, you had more faith in me than I could ever possibly have. Thank you for that loud knock on the shut doors of my heart.

My love and gratitude to my beloved aunt, Rosenda, who kept 'pulling my right strings' at the right time. Without your unwavering faith in me, I wouldn't have made it this far. From the cover design to the title, from the sight to the breath, you have been in me and in every page of this book.

Make hay while the sun shines. I couldn't have asked for my sun to shine more brilliantly and at just the right time! Sana, I value your presence in my life deeply.

Mama and Baba, my heart and my soul. "You are not meant for nothing." The power of these words made me believe. "You are our booin, our Chinar." I hope I become one, some day.

Junaid, whom I love a million times more than I express, whose heart shall always be connected to mine.

My namesake, Saba Mahjoor, who nudged me to keep writing and keep believing, I cannot thank her enough for the kindness she showed to a stranger.

Hafsa, the loving sister I never had, who gifted me her spectacular photographs, Momin, my friend, my accomplice, Afnan, my kid brother, Ma, Daddy and the rest of the family, for all the love and warmth they have showered upon me, thank you a million times over. Justine, who holds the mirror up so gently for me, nudging me to keep looking in it, many thanks for giving me your hand each time I fell. Othman, my dear friend, my very own 'physician,' who urged me to keep churning it out, my thanks to you as well. A bouquet of gratitude to my grandparents, my uncles and aunts (both sides of both the families!) and all my cousins for their valued presence in my life. Gratitude to Dr. Wahid Khan who listened to me, no matter what, no matter when. Sabzar, my other brother, who has been a blessing in this life.

A big thank you to Judy for putting together the beautiful cover of the book.

Gratitude is due to Miss Farina Gailey and Mr. Pohar Baruah for their timely assistance in getting this book published.

Last but not the least, to all those who read this book, I hope you find the journey as meaningful as I did.

Saba Shafi.

Delhi, 17 March 2017.

When you give someone the weapon to destroy you and still believe with all your heart that they won't, and there you see the dagger being plunged right into your heart, you feel no pain. Absolutely none. Instead, you smile peacefully.

Words of ambiguity, half formed sentences, meaningful pauses and deafening silences. Who makes the effort of writing these out on crumpled sheets of paper? Who makes the effort of articulating silences and passing them over to another realm of dreadful silences?

Who else but the broken? Who else but the broken?

So here she was again, addressing her silences in words.

And here I was…trying to extrapolate her words from her silences, reading her letters for the umpteenth time.

"The sadness will last forever."

Suicide note, **Vincent van Gogh**

The Lost Letter to Kashmir

26th March 2016
Delhi

Dear Sun,

There is a lot of darkness inside me, of which you have no idea. It hurts me beyond repair at times, so much that I feel as if my heart might implode. I cry it out. How long have I been trying to cry it out now? This river doesn't seem to dry up. We have deluge upon deluge upon deluge. And here I am inundated again, heart, soul and mind drenched in the torrential rains. I know I'm doing something terribly wrong, which is why the anguish returns.

I was asked today if I felt angry. Angry at the world? Angry at everyone? Angry at myself? Perhaps I do. But what good is impotent anger that incapacitates your own being? Hell is of our own creation, Sun. And in choosing this I'm choosing hell. Nay! I'm creating hell for myself and those that are inadvertently connected to me. I want to disentangle myself from this web. And I know I will. I will. I will. One day. Not very far away. It will all end, and the pieces will then fall in place and I will begin to understand the bigger picture which seems elusive now. I'm baffled, yes. I am running away, yes. I fret too. But even this will go away just as the sun sets down each night. Someone asked me today, why do you seek teachers? Why can't you be a teacher? It makes me think now. We are teachers and students, both. Perhaps I'm a bad student when life decides to teach me a thing or two. And now I'm an even more impatient teacher, for I am unable to teach myself important lessons on kindness and compassion. I don't credit myself with much. Why do you think? It was suggested it might be because I seek validation from others. Do I, I wonder? On a good day, I probably know I'm well. On a bad day, I simply go ten feet under the ground and cannot even crawl. And the bad days have been stretched a tad bit too long now.

The fire of my rage, if that's what it is, only singes my own heart and thus, I must rid myself of it. I am trying. I'm trying. I will keep trying. There is so much that needs to be erased. So much trash in my head. I want to curl up like a tiny bud and open slowly, petal by petal, all over again.

Giving up is not an answer, I know. It's an easy escape. One ought to accept the difficulty one is faced with, no doubt. Like you say, one mustn't resist one's state. But once accepted, one must look for tools to overcome the hurdle. Jump over the obstacle. In writing to you, Sun, know this-I only write to myself. In my heart and mind, there must be no room for fear, don't you think? No room for anger or hatred. Whatever it is, that shackles my heart must become the key to unfetter the locks too. In the heart of every problem is hidden the solution. One only needs to shake oneself up and keep looking. Keep looking hard. Or perhaps, close ones' eyes too sometimes. And let the answer find you. Else, let the peace of unanswered questions reverberate within. 'Answers without the right questions,' like you often say. We can exist with holes in our being, after all. In fact, they are good for us. They make us light, buoyant and well aerated. It is through these gaps that light reaches us, I am told. I must believe what He tells me. He teaches us using contrasts, many a times. Darkness is nothing but a harbinger of light. Dusk, blends into night, only to be broken by the crack of dawn. Sorrow helps us appreciate and value joy when we feel it. Tears prepare the soil for smiles that have already been sown. They only water the seeds that will sprout very soon. Hope. Strength. Call it what you may, Sun. The goal is the same. To hold on tightly. To show up each day. To be steadfast even when one is crumbling from within and to wait for the light to ignite our being from inside.

You know why I write to you? And how I'm probably able to say a lot, even though I might not be saying much directly? Because I feel understood. And that's quite a nice feeling. You know what my mirror told me today? My mirror told me that the heart always moves in a direction where it feels a pull of love. That is so true. And what better an act to keep your heart in its rightful place by simply learning to love oneself? That, by no means, is easy I realize. But then, what is easy in life? Nothing of value, wouldn't you agree?

I must bid you adieu now, for night invites me to put my head softly in her lap. I wish you a gentle night as well, filled with peace and solace.

All my love,
S.

After reading this, anything but peace and solace would beckon the night.

Prologue

He kept repeating his name feverishly over and over again, breaking into cold beads of sweat each time he woke up in the middle of the night, his name and his address, repeatedly as if he were possessed by some demon, some djinn, rocking his body back and forth, nursing his own heart, shielding and protecting it, trying his best to create a safe haven when everything around seemed to be dicey and shaky. As he na`rrated this incident to her about five years ago, she had cowered down and had simply wanted to run out on him. She had thought him to be mad. In hindsight, she now realized that she had understood that 'madness', recognizing it as scarily familiar and it had evoked such immense fear in her, that she had wanted to sprint out of that potentially damaging relationship. Two bad swimmers can never make it to the shore, her subconscious seemed to be telling her. "Run, run, run! He is just as insane as you!"

Five years on, as she was rocking herself to some degree of calm, as she kept wringing her hands continually, he had stood his ground firmly. His instinct was not to run for his life or run for cover, he wanted to pull her out instead, no matter what, no matter how. He was perseverant to the point of being a pain in her neck, both literally and figuratively! Yes, his patience ran thin quite often and then one could spot flying saucers in their room, hairbrushes being hurled across each other (its broken handle a reminder of his anger antics) and spectacles being smashed against the wall. A tongue that was hardly used caustically had been the worst casualty of this tamasha that unfurled each day. No, he wasn't a smooth talker at all, he wasn't crafty with words, yet that poor little vestigial organ was most cruelly used, abused, bruised and battered. Each time she drove him to a point of insanity, he bit his tongue in a fit of rage, quite literally, in the hope of saving himself the trouble of spewing venom on her. Verbal vitriolage wasn't his cup of tea (he hardly ever drank tea either, much to her dismay!). He had become her punching bag and she was no less than Muhammad Ali, only that she rarely ever floated like a butterfly, though she quite often stung like a bee!

This was the five hundredth time in five years that they were trying to lay down the rules of a separation. No, they were both cowards they decided, hence their cowardice prevented them from going downhill. Instead, he proposed, that they keep the facade of a farcical relation, while she would be allowed the liberty of kindling other flames. She could be a libertine while he would practice 'Omerta.' Easy-peasy!

She kept listening to these words, reminding herself that he was only letting off some steam and didn't mean a word of what he said.

And then, suddenly he broke down. He just couldn't see her stagnate like that, wasting herself, letting herself wilt and wither, doing nothing except washing clothes, doing the dishes and mopping the floor. If getting out of each other's lives would help her get back on her feet, so be it, he said level-headedly. His earnestness and desperation stunned her. It was the same desperation that she had seen in him as he had immersed himself in his work, the same mad angst with which he had back then, rocked his body, and was now expressing his anguish in slow, measured, rhythmic tones. "Get out of here, go back to Kashmir, go back home!" he mumbled. She suppressed her desire to let out an angry sigh. "Ours wasn't a 'normal' relationship anyway," he went on. Not by any stretch of imagination. It

16

was an aberration right from day one. A horrible experiment gone horribly wrong. There had been no 'chemistry,' no 'fireworks,' no 'effervescence,' no 'mental challenge,' no 'power play', no 'fatal attraction' and no 'tickling of her gray matter.' And it was becoming increasingly clear that none of it mattered. Gray. White. Or black.

He was to be her death. An anathema, her anti thesis. He was snuffing out all her ideas about love, life or her own self. He was doing to her emotionally, what the megalopolis, Delhi, had done to her physically and mentally. He was tipping her off balance. She was forced to stand up and admit that she no longer knew what she truly stood for, what her core beliefs were, where her center of gravity lay. She had just been born and was quivering nervously. Desperately holding onto her ideas of familiarity when her exterior was showing such tectonic shifts, she was only trying to recreate the same false sense of security as he had tried to, all those years ago as he kept repeating his name over and over to himself. This was an epiphany. The idea had struck her on the terrace of a cafe, under the starry sky. And it was, now, as they walked together in the park that she could give it some form, some structure, a voice. She had been pining for the Chinar leaves where the Ashoka trees stood tall, she had wanted her shikara rowing where the Ola plied. She had been looking for 'sameness,' for the comfortable blanket of familiarity. She kept chanting breathlessly over a rosary, hoping for mountains to be conjured up where concrete jungles stood tall. And now she understood it all. She needed to let the Chinar stay where it was, with its roots buried deep in the damp soil of her soul and the crunch of its crimson autumnal leaves resonating with her heart, but she had to let the Banyan tree grow side by side as well, it's roots intertwining with the Chinar, locked in a friendly embrace. The temperate and the tropical could coexist, the chill of snow and the oppressive summer heat could melt into each other's arms. Only if she allowed such an unlikely communion to take place. And who knows what other trees might root themselves in her heart: Maple, White Oak and Paper Birch?

But for this she had to bare herself more fully and that's what seemed to be happening. All her elaborate garments were being ripped off and she

17

stood naked, shivering in the freezing cold, sweating in the sultry sun all at the same time.

And she kept wringing her hands and scratching her head trying to make some sense of what had hit her.

When you are stripped off your very identity, what do you do? When it suddenly dawns upon you that your idea of The Truth is not the only truth but only a tiny fragment of the multitude of truths, what do you do? Your ego senses a radical transformation in the offing, an antigenic shift of pandemic potential, perceives it as a threat and resists it ferociously, mounting a robust immune response against this vile 'other,' the 'foreign invader,' shutting down completely, inexorably. Her id, ego and super ego were in a pandemonium and she had hit a dead end. She was frantic, she was gasping for air, flailing her arms wildly as her insides were being churned and tossed from one end to the other. She had been unfavorably disposed to such a tumultuous tempest and was feeling nauseatingly sea sick. Yes, her little boat, her shikara had capsized and she was no swimmer. Neither was he. So that kept any hopes for her heroic rescue at bay. She was playing the part of a 'damsel-in-distress' quite well but he was just not her quintessential 'knight in shining armor.' How could her fairytale have gone so terribly wrong! Just how! Not even were her tresses long as his sleepless nights, for she was no Rapunzel.

Her predicament was echoed by Amir Khusro's lament,

'Shabaan-e hijraan daraaz chun zulf, wa roz-e waslat cho umr kotah'

Long as her tresses unravels the night of separation, short as life is the day of communion...

Love had the nasty power of tossing over the sturdiest of us. Her supposed 'love affair' with 'intellect,' that fancy fantasy of an imaginative mind, was breathing its last, as she, very consciously, was feeling a palpable shift in her thermal set point- a shift from the head to the heart.

Having been told that incessant scratching of one's head signified a desperate attempt to open the lid of ones overly active mind as against biting one's nails which was meant to release the pressure off one's heart, she had started doing the latter. She wanted to make sure that she chose mind over matter and heart over mind any day. She just had to be connected to her heart more than she was with her head. She could think with her head alright, but she could love only with her heart. Whether it came instinctively or not, whether she was to condition an unconditioned reflex or not, she simply had to set the balance right. Either her scalp scratching had to stop, or her nail biting had to increase. Nature loved order, balance, equilibrium, harmony, while she was perpetually going towards a state of higher entropy, disorder, chaos, confusion. Homeostasis. Yes, that's what would cure her-a steady state, an open exchange. She needed to let her body breathe and breathe freely. She let out a sigh. Azadi! Freedom! That's what freedom would mean to her. She couldn't keep inhaling her own stale, vitiated air, she needed to go over to the other side of the fence where the grass was still green, and the land seemed virginal.

She was no mystic, no recent convert, not even an overenthusiastic zealot, but this seemed to be the closest that she could get to annihilation of self in her own humble way. She was finally 'laying down arms.' She was putting her head down against the lumpen mud of her existence and admitting that she didn't know anything, that she no longer could tell. She had no opinions, no fixed ideas and no preconceived notions. Nothing! Absolutely nothing! She would keep arriving at a new zero, a new cipher, each time she completed one full circle. This was how she was to circumambulate the Kaaba of her own existence. She had to stand on top of it, with her soiled feet and soul, disregarding its structural sanctity, rejecting its tendency of being reduced to a mere symbolic potential idol, refuting and repudiating her own ego worship and emphasizing its nothingness resoundingly! This was what her call to prayer was to be. And this inner muezzin hardly needed any validation from the outer world. It had no need to count heads that would prostrate in love and devotion, for the only head to touch that moist earth ought to be hers.

This was to be the beginning of her story, her zero, her all....

19

"I have been shown in darkness, light + have learned that even in prison, one can be free. I am grateful. I have come to see that there is good in every situation, sometimes we just have to look for it. I pray each day that if nothing else, you have felt a certain closeness + surrender to God as well +have formed a bond of love + support amongst one another…"

Kayla Mueller
American aid worker in Syria

Kashmir, 8 July 2017.

A militant rebel leader, Burhan Wani, was shot dead by the Indian armed forces in a remote Kashmiri village. The killing sparked a series of spontaneous demonstrations and protests, which, in a matter of day, turned into a popular revolt against Indian dominion over this disputed state. A bloody summer left many children blinded, thousands injured and killed about a hundred.

Chapter 1

The City of the Blind

"Write! Write! Write it all out!"

The urgency in his tone had been glaringly palpable. His voice had burst forth in brief flashes through the telephone, as she kept clinging tremulously onto it. She had been hit by *'the malady.' Yet again.* And his message had been brief and telegraphic, but it had carried immense depth and import in its seemingly cryptic code. A method to contain and channelize all the madness. That is what she had been advised to seek. With such insanity on display in the streets of her home, in Kashmir, it was impossible not to crumble, impossible to stay afloat. Dotted lines, slanting, seductive curves and broken fragments of her fractured imagination- these were to be her panacea. When the outside world seemed hopeless and despairing, one could only hope to create a false sense of security inside, for it was impossible to detach oneself from the darkness that was slowly creeping in from all sides, impossible to keep one's eyes open when children were being blinded blatantly, impossible to save oneself from the shadows that kept lurking all around, in each corner of the deserted streets of a ghost city- a city of the walking dead, fast becoming a city of the blind.

"Write!" he had reiterated, frantically." Let loose those caged birds fluttering desperately in your head, swirling, soaring around in circles, reaching the glorious zeniths above and plummeting the darkest depths below." The whole world could be traversed in one bold, insane flight of imagination. *Insanity*! That was the only prerequisite for it. And that was one resource that seemed to be in such an abundant supply as to somehow manage to renew itself each time one cycle of madness ended. Wild birds clashing with each other, colliding head on, almost bursting into flames, rolling, resurfacing, returning, reforming. To somehow forget the reality of life as they had known it, she had to write!

Write till the eyes remained.

"Write! Write! Write!"

"What you don't create will end up destroying you. So, dig it all out. Dig! Dig! Dig deep down! Dig it before it digs out your grave!" His voice had ended abruptly as if someone had snapped out that nerve just after the message had been delivered. *Barely*. A sudden flash and then no more. Darkness!

She could very well have been asked by some cruel twist of fate to make a tiny, precise, neat and clean nick in her own artery to let out her pain. Radial, perhaps (if she were tentative and timid), or higher up in her brachial if she were bold and daring. But plain *mad* as she were, you could almost, by very little cajoling and even less of thought ask her, as if by sheer magic, to dig deep with those tiny, ugly nails straight into her own heart and rip it open. *Right through the center*.

Writing signified bleeding, it exsanguinated her completely. Writing was sacred, sacrosanct. It was a pact entered, with one's own spirit; an arduous, laborious surgery one performed on oneself, or so she naively thought. A cardiac bypass conducted upon one's own heart, if you may. She scratched her head in agony. If only we could free ourselves from the narrow confines of fancy, empty, hollow words! How she detested the clunking noise they made as she checked them for meaning and veracity, for depth and profundity, with her pale knuckles striking against their shallow skulls! *Knock.... knock...Rap...Rap...*All pomp and show gone, all flair and flourish robbed off, all flesh and muscle ripped apart, the skeleton of those empty, dented words stood ugly in their stark nakedness. What she subsisted upon, hence, was an osmosis of her soul. Simply put, she had to let forth a gush of blood from her heart, with such maddening velocity, such supersonic speed to shake the very foundation of her existence with its mere impact. The whole world could then be reduced to rubble in one swift blow, like a deck of cards coming crashing down, falling one atop the other. Crumbling. Disintegrating. Degenerating. Decaying.

And there she stood amid those ruins....Blind ghosts sleep-walking through a graveyard of soiled memories.

How she came to such a pass each time, was a mystery she hadn't even *begun* to unravel. Not yet. One cursed moment, one bolt and there she fell...tripping on the elaborate, messy folds of the tapestry of her carelessly laid out, scattered words...

This mutation came unannounced, as everything else of any remote significance. *Accidentally*, almost. A stumble, yet another fall. A shocking, astounding discovery of a Frankenstein monster, sitting all along in our cozy drawing rooms until a barely audible rustle of the autumnal *Chinar* leaves brought it *blindingly* into the realm of our consciousness. Nerves were then stretched out (optic it was this summer), laid open on the roads, taut, high strung, ready to be plucked, quivering and aching almost! Faces contorted -gory, grotesque masks stretched snuggly across impassive faces, awaiting death. Molten fused lava being made one with the skin, burning it, searing it, ready to be ripped apart, mask and skin alike.

Writing was no pleasure trip to *Neverland*. Not here. No happy sojourn, no merry making, no flippant business, no careless carousal. It was, brutally put, a careful excision of the soul. Slow and painful. Self meeting self, self destroying self: words annihilating existence. It was Death unto itself. A macabre dance. A repetitive cycle of dying, mourning, scavenging ravenously on one's own flesh, charred a burnt black by long spells of self-deprivation.

"And in this death, would come mercy." Or so she ranted madly......

For what she wouldn't create would eventually destroy her...

So, she dug her grave, laid down her battered body in it softly, closed her eyes and murmured...

Live, die and live again....

For this was the *City of The Blind* now...

"Don't do this...don't, please, no... no... please" …

There was this lake of washed-out memories and then there was her own Dal lake, the water, calm and serene, agitated now and then by the sifting of bodies buried underneath, fish, algae, migratory birds, the clap of oars cracking the glassy lake, disturbing the reflections on the surface, and love...

Her barge stood still in the middle of the water as the blue of the lake breathed in the silver of the sky. Silver and blue calmly enmeshed, adorned with the pearls of ripples and currents, without any ironing, the creases exposed on the surface flashing the golden of the houseboats. This was it. Her love. She craned her neck to look deeper underneath the surface of the waters. A coffer of secrets would swim to her every now and then from the heart of the lake. She read it too well. Her lake. And there was her heart within the heart of this lake that had chosen to embrace her in silence. She sighed, looking out for the dark love hidden inside, buried within. She noticed the ruffling currents on the surface, and on a careful look, she could see the coarse figure sinking in those dark waters. No arms, no feet, no head-just the body: deformed, deranged, random, rough, and granular. The mighty sapphire mountains echoed her silence, her fear and her love. Sounds, whispers and murmurs wafting aimlessly started reaching her ears. And there was this sigh, too.

"You wish to fall in love?" the voice arising from underneath the surface of the lake asked.

She flinched back in horror. "Yes", she whispered plainly, her gaze affixed at the body underneath.

"But I have already fallen in love", she said, remembering him, smiling.

"You fall in love, yes. But you never flourish in love", the mellowed voice said. The smile vanished.

"What?" She asked trying to sieve the sense from the abstruse.

"There were stories and then there was love", the voice declared.

"I am not sure if I understand ", she stuttered

"You will, very soon", came the reply. She felt transfixed as if a hypnotic spell was being cast on her.

"I have fallen in love, trust me, I have," she kept repeating, as her barge started rocking in the waters.

A high-pitched laughter resounded from all sides, emanating from within the black waters, the voice grew louder and louder, and then toned down, lower, fainter, distant, drowning.

"HELP...help....help," the voice echoed. She extended her arms to help the body, to pull it out of the water. But it had no arms for her to clasp. No arms. Her heart sank at this.

"Who are you, please, please tell me?" she begged in a tone of urgency, as the body drowned deeper and deeper, the distance in between ever expanding.

Silence engulfed her existence as the chilly wind rising from the waters brushed against her dimpled cheeks.

And then the voice answered as it grew distant, "Love, love, love.... love......love...l o v e...", the voice drowned out into the silent depths of the lake. *You fall in love, you never flourish in love*

"Why did you do this, why, come back...see"...

My lake has frozen I am told

Frozen in those chilly wintery nights

the nights when sleep evaded me

How many were they? I know not

My eyes turned blind could not see

I lost all count

of night and day

Somewhere along, I lost my way

only to find one fine morning

that the waves on my lake had ceased to be

The *shikaras* waltzed on that surface no more

Those gentle, graceful rides were frozen too

That *splish-splash* had stopped

For my lake had frozen once more

And with it were stilled so many folklores

So many songs lay buried under that ice

How many hearts were cold too?

How many searched for warmth in you?

Did youthful hearts filled with hope

skate on that thin sheet of ice?

Did their feet draw figures on it?

Sharp blades tracing their hearts on ice?

Did laughter echo on the surface still

though silence was buried deep inside?

Can warmth penetrate those icy cold hearts?

Can love still make its way in?

once all softness had frozen within?

Can joyous *shikaras* still glide past

spreading ripples of happiness in the heart?

Could we hope for the hope of a blessed ride again?

Or would it all be in vain?

For my lake had frozen yet again...

The year was 1992. A little girl, all of five then, could not contain her joy as her parents took her to show the 'lake' for the very first time in all those years. She gasped in excitement, breaking into peals of laughter, looked at her mother, wide eyed and pleasantly surprised. 'Where had you hidden this all along? How come I get to see it now?' she questions them, in a tone that did nothing to contain her overflowing happiness, also one that brought to the fore a deep, boring sense of hurt, deprivation and betrayal. Yes, they had cleverly hidden all beauty and joy that she ought to have inherited being born here, instead burdening young shoulders under the immense weight of fear and uncertainty. She felt cheated, tricked, duped, in fact. Who decided what they must inherit from this land? How? And why? Were they asked what they wished for?

Many years later, as they spent yet another year in a beautiful mental prison, a loud noise is enough to make them lunge forward and crawl on the ground. Yes, this was one emergency drill that had been inscribed in their DNA by now. All loud noises were ominous, unless proven otherwise. Kneeling on the ground on all fours, they crawled away from the windows, only to realise the folly of their act. What cowardice! A firecracker had been mistaken for a shot fired in the air, the thick menacing soot settling on their mottled lungs having turned black from years of mental bondage. They had exchanged their shiny glass bangles for iron shackles that fettered their minds inexorably. What an unfair deal! Occupation occupies the mind. Nay! It consumes it. The fire spreads far and wide, in the uneven terrain of one's psyche, until sharp, jagged peaks are thrown up, those unscalable heights that must be conquered, whether one liked it or not. There was some truth in it after all. Conflict was cancerous. It spread and grew at an alarming rate, depriving one of all nourishment, until it wasted one's mind, body and soul. And they were the treacherous 'children of conflict,' as they had been romantically christened, at a time when there was no love lost left for their land.

As one's mind is bombarded with images of fearless young kids holding stones in one hand and a death wish in other, one is forced to address a few uncomfortable questions. 'How do you feel seeing an entire generation harboring a collective death wish?' These words voiced by a stranger, pierced through the phone, penetrating her, as she lay embroiled in a tempest, making sense of pain, both personal and collective. In a fused, syncytial 'existence,' where is the 'line of control' that separates individual from the collective? Surrounded by mountains on all sides, cut off from the rest, the valley is so designed that whatever rock is cast only ricochets back onto us. No matter whose hands releases it, the ones to loosen their grip on life is us. Ours.

My stones hurled against your bullets, you say?

The warm, moist softness of my child's palm

against the cold, coarseness of your hands?

My fate against yours?

The slow, sinuous, tentative, treacherous lines

fading abruptly into the dark chasm of nothingness

My hopes spread down gently like a carpet,

trampled upon by the Boots of Tyranny

My voiceless voice, pleading, beseeching, wailing, moaning

All life shrunk and compressed into a *Shahtoos* shroud--

--your youth and mine

passed swiftly, through the cruel Ring of Fate

My stones hurled against your bullets, you say?

My earthen *kangri* against your hellish Hearth of Fire?

My crimson rivers against your blood turned white?

Cruel orders barked or my animal cries?

Arms twisted and turned behind my back

The cold, black metal stretched against my skin turned deathly white in terror

Seeing deaths of my children's children

Unborn, they die.

My womb, their graveyard

My body, a cage

My stones hurled against your bullets, you say?

Reality hit her too harshly.

Its music was too jarring for her delicate ears. It sent her head in a tizzy, whirling at lightning speed, twisting, pulling and rotating it mercilessly-rapid pirouettes performed in opposite directions-until everything came to a screeching halt. Oh yes! She had nailed it finally! This is what her perennial ache boiled down to. She had arrived at this diagnosis after several tormenting brushes with 'the malady' as she had coined it flippantly, when such flippancy could be afforded at all. Such close shaves, such sudden collapses, such sharp plummeting descents as she suffered! Life almost reaching the brink of her cold, marbled lips in such moments, only to be hysterically inhaled back in one sudden gasp. One yank and one fierce pull.

To stand on that uneven cliff repeatedly was such an ordeal for her. And even more trying for those that helplessly looked on. This precipitous fall could be fatal for her. Biting their hands frantically, fighting with all the courage they could summon, they leapt out to grab her hand, pulling her back in one desperate, swift movement.

A hopeless flapping of limbs -this struggle against the harshest of currents, pulling one deep down. Oh, the lifelessness one feels, the weightlessness in that fraction of a millisecond before the body slowly slackens, easing out, light and limp. That final act of letting go. Of simply opening one's arms, embracing life and death. *Life in death.* That acute awareness of feeling each tiny molecule coursing through every little pore of one's skin. "One is most alive in the moments leading up to one's death", she theorized with a gentle, resigned tilt of her head. After all, sensations were heightened when juxtaposed with stark, glaring contrasts. Love. Hate. Rise. Fall.

Life...Death

Light...Darkness

The thought of losing life to death would suddenly, almost shockingly jolt her out of her reverie. There was too much of that happening around her anyway! Life existed *still*, and every inch of her being clung onto it with such force as can be known only to the dying. To bend and break oneself and then hunt madly for those scattered parts, uncertain hands groping at unidentified halves, grabbing whatever came within their reach, touching it, feeling her way around it, sniffing at it to bring forth to memory any smell of distant familiarity, smells assimilated into her being. The smell of childhood-of hands dirtied in mud, the redolent smell of rain falling on the chiseled rocks of her balcony, *devier kani*. How she had loved it! How her tongue would reach every little crevice, each tiny fissure of the rain kissed stone, sipping innocently, coltishly, tongue rolled up forming a shallow spoon, slurping noisily, sipping away the joys of childhood, that sweet nectar of innocence.

A distant voice snapped her thread abruptly, leaving behind fast receding, fading trails in the dark, narrow alley of her memory. A memory that belied her history. A memory that cast its menacing shadow on her present. A memory that tarnished all hopes of future.

"...Come back. Come back," he whispered in her ear. "See, your lake is still here."

Everyone else had a thing or two to tell her to simplify her 'condition.' Everyone, except herself, knew *exactly* what was wrong, what ailed her and could deftly trace the entire temporal sequence of events leading up to her present 'state.' Her real problem, among myriad others of course, was that she was the vile possessor of an unfeeling heart. This nail was repeatedly drilled inside her hardened skull and an even harder heart, crackling through it, boring its way into that hard boiled, ruthless, callous blackened stone that she was accused of possessing. That brutal, cold inanimate object with tiny sharp daggers of icicles dripping from her frozen chest. She was mocked, derided and scorned at for such unforgivable lapses in her being. Ah! The utter darkness of the soul! What 'blinding' misery!

But what confused her utterly *then*, was how each barb could find its way so easily, so effortlessly, into that insensate organ that she was accused of harboring. No matter how high and impenetrable the walls of this fortress that she had built around herself, one unkind word was enough to bring it crumbling down, razing it to dust and rubble. Such was her vulnerability at one level, one that she hid from all scrutinizing, judging eyes. But those that had skimmed her surface, broken past the hard shell and reached the center, her milky white kernel, knew and understood her in her enormous frailty.

She was a paradox, her head and heart in a 'state' of constant 'strife,' one shouting over the other, one blocking and silencing the other, a perpetual, tiring hide-and-seek, a battle of un-equals. It drained her, tormented her, and shook her from deep within. It was a source of constant mental, emotional and spiritual fatigue, a festering wound, fingered cruelly by those that understood it not, but whose lives were impossibly sucked into this ravaging, wild fire. Dejected and defeated, she fancied wallowing in her misery for once. She could do it for a second and no more, for very soon she found herself guilty of every crime committed upon every other soul, save her own. Such acute awareness terrified her!

It simply made her want to loosen her grip on life, to let go, to stop swimming fiercely against the dreadful, frightening currents that rocked her exhausted body from this end to that. All she wanted to do was to extend her arms fully now, with complete abandon and embrace whatever the high rising, frightening waves brought in their wake.

And in such frangible moments of utter darkness, of absolute surrender, was born a hope. A hope of being carried safely ashore.

To home, to heart…

Another disappearance, yet another attempt to escape. She found herself consumed by a desire of seeking righteousness in the world by wronging her own soul; hence, another attempt of inflicting pain upon the self. 'Why struggle when you can just be?' she would ask, each time she wrote letters of wrapped silences and unfulfilled hopes. Her fingers felt numb by the countless acts of tracing the inked letter to assess the intensity with which the words had been etched against the wrinkled paper, violating its plainness with its ironed curves of the cursive. Curse. Cure.

Dear Sun,

It's been a while since we last spoke. I don't know where the entangled mess, those threads laid threadbare lie anymore, but I attempt nonetheless. You must be wondering why the silence? I know you had been meaning to speak with me. I also know you believe me when I say I needed to speak with myself. And so, I write. And as I put to paper whatever has been roaring inside, waiting to gush forth, I take a conscious breath. Just the way I had been taught. I notice myself from a distance. I move beyond myself, far far away, and observe myself observing myself. Do I sound funny to you? I know you will smile 'with' me, and not 'at' me. And here it makes me smile again! See? Can you see that in this letter? Can you see that smile stealthily appearing in the curves of my words, peeping over the corner of my sharp edges, and settling in the creases of my eyes and in the tiny sparkling dots of my 'i's?

Why do I write to you? Why did I write to you then? Why do we wish to drown and still hope to be saved? Why can't I simply sit by the banks of the river and feel the icy coldness playfully touching my feet, one sensuous ripple after another? Why do I fling myself, heart and soul, immersed in those waves, hoping to somehow be carried onto another shore? And the pang of losing an old home revisits me again. Yet, it does not, in any way, deter me from jumping right in. I rush and rush and rush at dizzying speed to reach the very heart of the ocean, hoping to either be lost forever in its dark depths or float gently, weightless and bouyant.

As I pack boxes again, placing bits of my life in it, I know I must learn the trick all over again. It does discourage me sometimes. To have thought that you had come a long, long way. And learnt a few lessons too. To then find yourself quivering all over again. I weep as I see myself weep. I rock, nurse and console the child inside. I embrace vulnerability. I snuggly wrap it around myself, wrap myself around it too, deriving comfort in the thought that this would be my only light on days not half as bright. This would be my only home, my only refuge.

You know, I have always wondered. Where is that point where one's softness, fragility or vulnerability ends and brokenness, disarray, damage and derangement begins? When is it your strength and where does it become an unbelievably unbearable pain? As you swing from one extreme of the pendulum to another, you forget this completely. You forget that you are touching, kissing, feeling the center, albeit transiently, but it's there. Yes, it's there! In that split moment, when you are there, aligned, directed, present, but also more fully when you begin describing yourself in terms of the distance from the center. That becomes your locus…. all the various points that exist between you and your home, you and your center. All that- the darker nothings in between, the concrete somethings, the half despair, half hope, the silences or the songs, the destinations and the paths-all that becomes home. There is merger, dissolution, formation and assimilation in it. It starts, it peaks, it plateaus and then it dips. See, the smile? It dips, yes it dips. And there we are wet all over again, awash with a new set of fleeting, evanescent emotions, ready to be flung away from the center all over again, our distance increasing our yearning, our love solidifying, cementing, flowing, rock solid, sweet as honey, a bitter poison, wildly enthralling and excruciatingly exacting! I am learning the drill, am I not? But just when I think I know, just when I let my body ease up, slowly uncurling my arms, feeling the breeze kiss my neck, just when I think I have learnt enough to let each tiny molecule resonate in tandem, coherently with my external, I face a churner. I clasp my heart wildly, in earnest, in desperation, in a maddening moment as I realize no cushion could cushion it ever! It must break, grow, mold and molt all over again. I keep staring at what is shed away, with no thought to spare...lonely songs sung in the dark, unfinished poems read in a delirious haze, sudden surges of tender love, sunny bursts of smiles captured in broken silver mirrors, tears smeared on dimpled, soft knees, the full arc of bright rainbows locked away in the arches of the lovers' feet. It is from underneath this brilliant awning that I write to you. Of love and lost homes. Of sanctuaries and deserts. Of drunkenness and desertions. Of aimless drifting and firm anchorage. Of breaths exhaled softly in the nights and the poems woven thereof.

I write to you from a place of love.

S.

Night goes back to where it was

Everyone returns home sometime

Night, when you get there,

Tell them how I love you....

- Rumi.

A war-torn country

'One hundred years of solitude'

An old rusty iron bed in a decrepit hospital

A wounded soldier

A vision in white nursing the wounds--

both his and her own

Shafi! Ya Shaafi al Amraz!

The intercessor, The Healer of all maladies

A tragic story conjured up in a fanciful head so full of stories!

A fable, a folklore--all head, no heart

Berating the fragility and wordlessness of all but her own

Could that be a parable that had the power to move

the staggering purple peaks, painstakingly chiseled?

Bare now, lush then.

Draped in a curtain of snow in the frozen winters

No whiff of saffron in the air

No wooly lambs chasing Mary across the azure skies

Dark now, scintillatingly bright then.

No *pashmina* tales woven

No silks flowing. No brocades donned

No ibex wandering. No gazelles in the Meadows

No Milton's *'Paradise Lost.'* No modern-day Hell

No bondage of the days of yore. No animals yoked together now

No trout exploding. Dismembered joints

A limb here. Throbbing in its search

A body looking for its dismantled head

No shoe there. Mary Janes at that

Little girls in pretty, white dresses with a tiny,

delicate buckle snuggling the soft, white ankles, refusing to let go

A dab of red sprinkled, splashed, as if from a pitcher of colors

The creamy, satin ear lobe with a tiny little turquoise stud

sparkling in it. *On* it. Now *through* the skin rendered transparent

The recalcitrant freckles on her high bridged nose

The curls in her hair. The waves in her heart

No songs long forgotten. No lamentations unheard

No sanguinity mixed in the emerald green waters. No *splish-splash*. No *plop-plop*

No *shikara* abandoned in the turbulent tide. No waves carrying the dead fish ashore

No trap. No triumph. No smoke from the snout of the samovar. No *kehwa* served

No Foucault in our sad, little boorish discourses

No henna in our coarse, wrinkled, veined hands. No wings spread majestically

45

No shade beneath this rotten *Chinar*. No concentric rings
circumambulating the center

Timeless. Ageless. Caught in its own intricate *jamavar*

No stories exchanged. No love transcending all barriers

No strange patterns made as drops break and join

as she slips her burnt, charred ankle in the cold *Lidder*

No shrieks. No laughs. No bosom touched. No floodgates forced open.

No *knock-knock*. No *clunk-clunk*

No cypress raising its arms plaintively

No apples, red, green and gold, weighing down the branches

No meeting of the earth below and the skies above. No horizon. No
sunset

No more *Veil. Vale. Wail.*

Carry this message, O westward wind…though the embers blaze no more

Yet to this home, I must return….

July 12, 2016

Insha, a fifteen-year-old girl from a small village in south Kashmir, was observing the clashes between protesters and armed forces in the streets from the window of her room, when the pellets fired to quell the stir, hit her, plunging her forever into unimaginable darkness.

She fiddled with her pen nervously. She knew she was jittery today. More than usual perhaps. She passed it from one hand to the other. As if this simple act of juggling a pen could suddenly create new ideas where none existed, construct bridges where none were possible, plant magical seeds in the once fertile soil of her mind-seeds that would sprout at the first hint of rain, and gardens would bloom, lush and green, kissed by the first shower-daffodils and narcissus would blossom, heralding spring.

There! She had nearly convinced herself with her words, lulling herself to sleep, when her eye caught the images flitting across the television.... *Blinding despair* on display on the streets of Kashmir. Children as young as eight were being blinded on the streets of their home. She felt a kick in the pit of her stomach, her pain was so acute, so visceral, so dark!

Again, she snuffed out all the barely lit candles of hope…

Glum, morose, disconsolate. That is how she would paint her present emotional landscape. She turned her sad little head around and observed the dimly lit room, taking in each minute detail of her new surroundings, making scraggly mental notes, absorbing, assimilating all that she could, in this one moment. "All this, *too,* was being etched in my memory," she thought. To be retrieved later, perhaps? When the haze would have lifted, and some clarity attained. When the tide would have ebbed, and one could then venture along the shore, picking up ivory shells, putting them to one's ears, trying to figure out the meaning behind all this continuous clamor, this raucous, deafening din. As a little girl, she recalled the joy of holding that creamy conch against her tiny ears when she would coax her grandfather to let her hear it one more time. 'Seashell resonance,' it was called. She had read about it somewhere as she grew older, demystifying all that she had imagined as a child. The noise of the surroundings masqueraded as the waves of the ocean. And all along she had thought that the shell had somehow internalized the entire ocean in its belly. Just gulped it down. How childhood tales come crashing down when reality 'strikes,' she thought. *Strikes!* She shuddered at the mere thought of the word. Now as an adult, she opined, that this noise was important to fully appreciate silence. To befriend it, to revel in the calm of the ensuing quietude. The noise seemed to signal towards something-one finger raised, slightly hooked, a gentle wave. This was a beckoning into the unknown, no doubt.

She craned her neck forward to take in her surroundings more fully. What caught her eyes first were shoes neatly lined against a cream-colored wall. They were little soldiers standing attentively in a single row, taking their wearers to lands unbeknownst to them. Away from home, away from danger. Home was no longer 'safe', home signified danger now, she sighed sadly. How did they come to such a pass? *Why?* She forced her mind to focus back on the soldiers, no, shoes! She corrected herself. Yes shoes, arranged neatly in a row, worn out and tattered, some from continuous use, while others from a deeper bond formed with them in difficult times. After all, they were friends that had dragged and pulled her out, forcing her to walk ahead in life, when all she had desired was to stay crawled up in her bed. They were fellow travelers in fact, she smiled. If only they could tell tales of their journey. And hers, too.

Her gaze wandered aimlessly to her right. Haphazardly arranged on the table were jars of all possible shapes and sizes. All pushed to one edge, leaving the other end empty, waiting to be filled. A transparent sugar pot made of glass was perched right at the center with tiny cubes peeking at her, shyly. Amidst the jars containing pickle and jams and lime juice, lay her personal favorite--an indispensable reminder of home: an 'instant – mix' powdered *kehwa* (the green tea for all occasions back home) that instantly brought forth varied smells from her valley-of spring and autumn, well ground and powdered cinnamons, cardamoms and saffron. It was much more than an olfactory treat for her or even a mere gastronomic delight. She buried her nose in it so often, each time she yearned for home. One heaped-up spoon that would assuage her longing, transporting her to what was now a mere abstract idea in her head-that vague, nondescript notion of 'home' and here was its nostalgia laden whiff. Like all impressionable images captured in the mind's eye, it was prone to being overly romanticized. Everything, just about *everything*, seemed far more beautiful – home and now even darkness- in her head.

She knew her mind was wandering, trespassing and straying into 'out-of-bounds' territories, 'cantonment' areas, her own streets walled off by those rolled up, barbed wires spread like a mind-boggling maze. What were they called? Ah! Yes! Concertina! The first time she had heard the word she had busied herself conjuring up images of a musical delight, a well-orchestrated symphony with the audience shouting encore! "Silly me!" she laughed. Who would say encore to this kind of deafening 'music' she shuddered.

As she sat struggling with the sweltering heat in Delhi, she knew things were *burning* back home. At least the air conditioner worked here, while *there* not even the lungs could draw in enough of that divine air- air that had turned putrid from the smell of burnt rubber tyres, spilled, congealed blood, pellets showered piercing nascent eyes bereft of dreams, stones pelted in rebellion, in rage. And here, she was listening to which materials ought to be used for such a carnage. Wonder what Mr. Charles Goodyear would have to say to those that proposed rubber being used for this 'experiment?' The year *that* 'resolution' would see the light of the day, would be a 'good year' for Kashmir, only that there would hardly be any with eyes left! God! How badly she wanted to breathe! Her obstinate, intractable head was desperately trying to join two disjointed ends of her life together, trying hard to mix two immiscible parts of her soul, her yin and yang, her light with her darkness, hoping it would dissolve just as easily as a spoonful of powdered *kehwa* from Kashmir dissolving in the boiling water in Delhi. She smiled at the uncanny analogy of the situation. Well, yes humor sure helped! Humor could mock life even in the face of death. It was defiant and rebellious challenging life with no iota of fear, not even an inkling of what fear meant, much like those young boys, no more than eight or ten that she had seen mocking menacing men armed with guns.

Now, *that* was dark humor. She closed her eyes as if to recreate what fear of darkness truly meant. Perhaps, sitting *here*, so many miles away, she had become blindly inured to that blindness. She felt like a deserter, a defector, guilty of complaining about the 'oppressive' heat when the same word had entirely different connotations for those back home. She too had her own darkness to grapple with after all, didn't she? Didn't we *all?*

A sudden beep startled her, and she woke up with a jolt, leaving her slow, deliberate mental expedition behind her, unfinished and abandoned midway. The sound that had broken her train of thoughts came from a black, metallic kettle. The water had boiled and was now ready. She looked down at her feet dangling from the chair, planted them firmly on the ground beneath and got up swiftly. Putting a spoonful of that white powder in boiling hot water, she sipped her *kehwa* slowly, feeling the subtle taste of saffron fields on her tongue.

Tonight, I pine for pines and conifers

For sapphire skies neck-laced with mountains

Tonight, I long for those tall cypresses

that swayed and danced in the playful breeze

For seasons that changed with the shifts in my heart

I wonder if they have forgotten me, being far away

So far away, yet so near...

My brackish tears had once dissolved in those rivulets

opalescent pearls homed in those homely oysters

And one sudden pull, one tug, a wrench, an exile imposed

That precious string of pearls now ripped apart

tiny beads of iridescent words lying scattered on the cold marble floor

Fractured hopes, broken promises,

dreams exhaled from lusterless lips

laid open and bare, again and again

Music stolen, poetry defiled, laughter robbed off

tales of tragedy shared with one and all

Raiment grabbed, passed from hand to hand, snatched and torn

thrown into the arms of my beloved lake

How *much* must it carry? How *much* will it contain?

No river this vessel of mine, that flows,

bends, leaves and carries

on her shoulders both poetry and pain

No river this one that sings and dances

as it forgets along the way

Such a fool this river of mine!

It stays, stagnates, sediments and chokes up

beneath the staggering silt of soiled memories

While I?

I sit silently along its banks, head bowed down,

bewildered, ashamed

What a vile temptress this creature of my mind!

enticing, alluring, seductive, but frail

What heavens were promised on these trails!

A defeated, gnawed at, corroded heart is all that remains.

My *Chinar* blazes no more--it's dried up, withered leaves fall

Landscapes change--her vacillating heart and you

A mausoleum of surrendered memories stands now,

where gardens had once bloomed

Deserted… Dilapidated… Doomed…

A fairytale lived inside a fairytale, a lie within a lie, realities changed, altered, sugar coated no more, as it was for her now, as it had been for *all of them*. Sharp, glaring images were dulled at the corners, pointed edges were smoothened, silhouettes were blurred and faded, blending with the surroundings, peals of laughter were amply amplified, silences were silenced forever, fires were being extinguished, tempers were tempered with, tweaked and tamed. No betrayals were agonizing anymore, no communions were rejoicing. Placid nothing is what she felt. If one were to ask her how her heart fared, she would fill deep gorges with her empty sighs. If you were to ask her whether her heart ached, she would only smile a sad smile, a masked smile, a veiled smile, draping in its folds and layers, all that she hid inside.

She was plagued- plagued by a constant, searing desire to chase air, catch it, hold it, mold it and even color it, all in her dreamy childlike innocence. But it slipped like a slimy fish, it always slipped right between her fingers each time she got close enough to feeling it, wrapping her hand around it, believing she owned it. She was naive. Vain too. A bit too dramatic, dare I say. She foolishly conjured up injuries inflicted upon her battered soul in her tiny little presumptuous head. Oh! She was silly and how!

Like all of them, she too desired freedom…. Freedom from her own thoughts…Freedom from the constricting confines of her own self…

Yes, her heart *did* ache. *Terribly so.*

On some days more than others. And this was no benign affliction that had gripped her. It was quite like wine, it aged with time, years adding to her grief, the fruitiness deteriorating slowly and the acidity increasing in incremental proportions, until her pain solidified and became more concrete. Her tears too, were being crystallized into rocks and stones, cast angrily at the world to bring down its 'order'…Her pang vaporized, and its odor became so permanent as to be a constant fixture that hounded her once proud little nose. "*That,* perhaps, was the reason for my perennially stuffy red nares," she surmised.

And Oh! Her darned imagination always ran wild! It was an unruly, wily beast that she found painfully hard to tame. Stubborn, independent, autonomous. It would take off into the wilderness without the slightest of hints. It was so quick on its feet! Such alacrity, such agility it displayed! Such a wide range of colors, a full arc of a rainbow spread across the rain-soaked skies, kissed only slightly by the tender, inchoate rays of the sun like an inexperienced lover fumbling over his beloved's body. It carried such beauty and rhythm that it made everything else seem inferior, inadequate and incomplete in comparison. Everything *paled* before the paleness of her mind, she chuckled.

Such fancy, fragmented 'figments of imagination' that she carried in her head were no less than a curse, one she knew she *had* to live with, just as she knew that she needed air to breathe, poetry to feel, a tinkle of laughter, a dab of kindness to feel alive and yes- stories to write…All over again.

Speak not of sadness tonight

For the eyes are tired now

And those rivers have all dried up

An endless barren desert

stretches between the two…

Home and heart

now thrown miles apart

Cold icy sighs exhaled,

still linger on as they depart

 resonating between the mountains and the lake

as exile upon exile is imposed

And no home remains home to her now…

She had foolishly picked up

a handful of soil from those lost lands

And held onto them, clenching her fists tight

And now?

That soil is turned to dust,

trampled upon by uncaring feet

To dust must she turn too,

only *then* could they meet…

So, mourn no more

shed no more tears tonight

Speak, thus, not of sadness tonight…

For the heart may be heavy

And the head empty

All silences may be silenced

and voice denied

Yet?

Yet, in this never-ending battle between

heart and the heartless

between words and the wordless

Emerges occasionally

from the depths of despair

those chilling shrieks

those animal cries

that could be muffled no more

so, I beg tonight, I implore

Speak of sadness no more...

for the pain becomes too much to bear

And those desperate pleas?

What heart could be strong enough to hear?

and still not break into a million pieces

the painful bits embedding deeper and deeper within

To *then* pull each shard out

and spread those scattered pieces

which pierce and penetrate

as desperate attempts are made to rejoin those ends

to reassemble, reunite

And *as* this war goes on, start not another tonight

Speak not...

Speak not of sadness tonight...

It was a cold hazy December afternoon. The heavy grey skies echoed her inner state more fully, the mist settling down heavily in the convolutions of her cerebrum, condensing in the nooks and corners of those carefully chiseled and carved out sulci-deep, wide, serpentine, and the dark, heavy clouds precipitate in these alleys, forming tiny rivulets. One tributary joins another and before you know it, the entire river flows in her head. The frothy, roaring cascades race at maddening velocity and she darts her eyes from one end of the street to another like a predator on the lookout for a vulnerable prey. The foam that is whipped in the gray zones of her brain escape the corners of her down-turned mouth as a short sigh. A black pashmina shawl is wrapped in several layers around her frozen head and melting thoughts, its blackness absorbing the overflowing darkness. She clutches her stomach and sprints across the lane. She catches her breath, gasping hungrily, greedily for air, each inhalation tormenting, each sigh painful. She enters the beautiful white house, oblivious of its sparkling stately bearing, aware of each prickly hair that stands erect on the nape of her strained neck. She is ushered up the stairs, her fingers holding the wooden railing, feeling the rotundity and the solidity of walnut wood against her sweaty cold palms.

Knock - knock...Knock - knock....

As her pale knuckles strike against the door, she hears a deafening rap against her cranium, right against her vault, in the hollow of her skull bones, crossing the suture lines at ferocious velocity. A tall lanky woman opens the door and she is smiled at and ushered in. She leans forward, dragging her feet against the wooden paneled floor and sits on the grey couch.

'Would you like some water? Warm or normal?'

Feeling the parched parchment paper-like lump in her throat, she nods her head in affirmation.

'Yes please. Warm,' she swallows painfully.

She is handed over a warm glass of water and she gulps the whole glass thirstily.

'How was your day?'

'Restless and foggy,' she says as she keeps moving her feet in to and fro repetitive movements.

Suddenly, she finds herself wringing her hands feverishly, as if desperately wishing to erase the lines that brought her here.

'My head hurts unbearably,' she moans holding her stomach instead.

As the images get blurred, breaking, dissolving, coalescing and blending with the darkness in the back of her bloodshot eye, she revisits the place in her memory. She stands by the edge of the river that rushed at breakneck speed then and bends over slightly to feel the temperature of the water that remained now, one little toe at a time. Yes, it is lukewarm and comfortable now. Comfortable for a swim.

Emboldened, she plunges more fully in the pool of her memory.

There she is. Back in the cozy room, sitting on the couch once again. She lets her gaze wander lazily across one corner and notices the white sheet that is spread across the bed...embroidered with colorful threads, the Kashmiri *crivel*, she recognizes with a smile. The room was softly lit, enclosed in a warm radiant glow of the yellow light emanating from the lamp placed carefully at the corner. The long wooden base of the lamp is hand painted, in delicate, bold strokes of pink and red and green dabbed at places by gold. Papier-mache. In another corner rests a table, the smell of freshly polished walnut wood wafting in her nostrils, the engraved Chinar leaves rustling in the lobules of her ears even when no breeze tickles it. On the desk rests a silver laptop, with half an apple shining through its back, the other half seemed to have been chipped off, nibbled away in one big bite.

She feels the penetrating gaze of blue eyes piercing through the whiteness of her eyeballs as a voice tugs her back from the lanes of her memory.

'What is your 'I'?' she is asked again over the phone now, as she sweats in the horrid heat of Delhi.

There is no right answer to this one she is told.

But the only right question to keep asking was this:

Where is your 'I?' What is your 'I?'

"There are days, hours, weeks, aye, and months, in which everything looks black, when I am tormented by the thought that I am forsaken, that no one cares for me. I assert that life is beautiful in spite of everything!

There are many thorns, but the roses are there, too."

-Pyotr Ilyich Tchaikovsky,
writing to his nephew about his battle with melancholy.

One day simply blended into another for her, one shadow expanding, compressing, shaping and reshaping. She hardly noticed the shifting patterns that light made on the floor of her room anymore, the unique dance that she had once loved. The paisley motifs, those geometric shapes, the dainty designs, that queer little mosaic of random images conjured up in her imagination. She was so much like a child that lay in the lush green grass on a beautiful sunny day and strained her eyes, imagining the strangest shapes in the cottony white clouds drifting overhead. She could see sad faces and smiling ones too, Cinderella's glittering shoes, Unicorns and nasty witches with long crooked noses. She could spend hours huddled next to the French window of her room, immobile, silent, keenly studying vague, abstract patterns that formed on the thick Persian carpet covering the floor, blending imperceptibly with those subtle hues, the paisley motifs, the almond blossoms, the stars spread out beneath her feet. Lost in this perusal, in these 'absence' spells, she would go far away from this world and its pressing engagements, onto another, transcending planes, sucked into a remote land, removed from her own. Her *own?* What *was her own* now? She no longer knew. But back *then,* at her home, Time and Space did not matter, for it would either freeze, motionless, calm and serene or gallop away at breakneck speed, in the blink of an eye. She couldn't tell which.

"Let go off my lappet!" her father had said gruffly as she kept clinging desperately onto his woolen gown, his dark grey *pheran,* moaning and wailing. As if, that would be the last rope that would ever be thrown her way, one that she needed to tug firmly at, lest life abruptly slips through her clumsy fingers. His guttural voice had reverberated in the room, the *hamam*-their heavenly hearth of long freezing winters where they huddled in comfort. That room had changed so much ever since. It had changed its *very* character, its *very essence.* From the erstwhile dark coffee hue of the walnut wood panels that ran vertically downward on those walls to the pale brown, unpolished natural shade of *deodar* (cedar) that now ran horizontally, making the room appear slightly bigger than it was, as if expanding its heart--a lot had changed. The tones had softened, as had the direction altered. Radically. Drastically. Irreversibly. It had acquired a more subdued bearing now. Yes, it had toned down, probably in the hope of admitting more light, once the dark, gloomy winters would give way to a fresh new lease of life in spring. That promised spring was still in the offing. It *had* to be somewhere, out *there*, within the reach of her fingers, no matter how awkward and gawky or tremulous they were now.

Despite the myriad changes it had undergone, some things had remained as they were, untouched and unsullied by the dirty waters that had flooded it a few years ago--that devastating deluge of 2014. One such constant that remained unchanged was the canopy that lay over her head. Those intricately connected pieces on the ceiling made a beautiful pattern, a repetitive sprinkling of stars intersecting circles--this astral, geometric design still shone in the darkest of her nights, somewhere far removed in her memory now. But she could still imagine and re-imagine, make and remake that pattern in her dreams. It had slowly seeped into her memory and spread in all her cells. How vividly did she remember it! Those small pieces of wood had been removed and rejoined painstakingly (thrice over now!), by master craftsmen using no more than their skilled hands, guided by unparalleled patience and unending endurance. It was a ceiling patterned like a jigsaw puzzle, the individual pieces finding their place, as if by sheer magic, fitting willingly, happily, of their own accord, like friends opening their arms to admit each other inside--locked in a tight, harmonious embrace. This was the starry sky underneath which they sat-- the *khatamband.*

It was under the protective shade of this stellar sanctuary that her father had told her, "Let go off my lappet! Hold *His*, not *mine*. I can do nothing. I will not be there for you forever. *He* will. I may not even listen, but He always will. He *always* does."

"Was He listening to my stifled sobs, as I tossed and turned restlessly, fighting the demons of my memory?" she mumbled to herself.

"Don't say that, please!" she had protested, sobbing uncontrollably.

"This is *the* truth, the *only* truth." had been his terse reply.

It was so typical of him! Having been exposed to the harsh realities of life at a very tender age, orphaned in his early teens, the oldest sibling among four, he was unbelievably pragmatic and worldly wise, yet *hopelessly* delicate and tender at heart, all at the same time. "My heart is like that of a woman's," he would whisper tenderly. And yes, he cried very often. He had cried as she had to leave her nest. How easy was it to move him to tears!

Today, as she felt that emptiness engulfing her again, she recalled his words laden with meaning. "Hold *His* lappet. No one else's."

For He *always* listens…. *Always*…

"How could all beauty have suddenly disappeared from my life?"

Whatever had happened to those childlike eyes, that innocence, the sparkle in the eyes, the twinkle, that devilish grin!

It wasn't that she had suddenly been *blinded* or that her eyes had been forced shut. It *was,* in fact, her heart that had been bolted, those doors being closed with a loud thud, forever. Her heart had simply wound up upon itself, rolling over and over, leaving no space, no nook or corner, no tiny crevice for any ray of light to steal its way in. No happiness seemed to be able to tip toe quietly, stealthily into that closed, dark chamber of hers.

Yes, that's what it had become now- a cold, dark chamber - and so she numbed her senses to feel no pain. It would all seem like one interminably long, long night, she thought and as dawn would break, (that first splash of orange and burnt fiery red spreading slowly, sensuously across the dark skies), she would remember nothing. *Nothing* at all! No tragedy would remain in her heart, no thorn in her finger, no sad songs would escape her lips, no remnant of that dry, painful lump in her throat, the lump that she went to bed with, each night. No disappointments would remain, no burning, boring, boiling, searing, scalding desires would overflow. *There would be no memory of any memory left.* She hoped for this gentle, rejuvenating breeze to blow away those dried, dead, shriveled up *Chinar* leaves. The leaves from Kashmir. She hoped for the wind to breathe new life into her, to dissipate all her angst and anguish away. She wanted to cast off this hard, toughened layer that had begun creeping in on her heart from all sides, adhering to it, those crooked, sticky, tenuous tentacles winding up around it, seizing it, clasping it forcibly.

This cage had to be broken. She knew it too well. Her soul had to be set free. It was inevitable. Liberation is what she sought. And this freedom had to come from *within*. She threw her head back, closed her eyes and a song reached her ears. A song of Hope. A song carried on the wings of a mighty magical bird. *A song of freedom....*

I long for a lush carpet of grass

under my bare feet

soft, moist, tender

The Pen that wrote it all down

long before the beginning of Time

The Pen that had inscribed all past

the present and the future too

The Pen that penned this Epigraph-

permanent and unchanging

The Pen that sealed broken fates

And crushed to dust all desires vain

Would it be that silent tears could fetch

drops from His Endless Ocean of Mercy?

Tiny driblets of Kindness and Forgiveness?

Of Love and Compassion?

mere trickles from that Vast Ocean

mere drops, no more?

Could it be that the solidness,

the constancy of those lines engraved,

would be revisited by the Magnanimity of His Grace?

One night, one night in a thousand and one nights?

Fates may be rewritten, relooked, they might?

Who knows which night might be that night?

When hearts would be aglow in His Sublime Light

One night, for sure... One night will come...

When the soul shall finally find a way out of all prisons

as was Jonah set free from his cage,

regurgitated back from the belly of the whale

when darkness was pierced by his earnest wail

One night... One night...

When arms would be flung wide

and the doors to hearts would be thrown open

Unlocked, unrestricted, unchained, unfettered

heads bowed down, in that wasteland,

in those desolated ruins

would *then* be raised gently in new gardens of bloom...

Someday... Some night...

It surely will come, only He knows when it might...

Someday... Some night...

One night in a thousand and one nights...

Chapter 2

Spring in Her Heart

Holding onto pain, all past and present, was tantamount to hugging the body of a beloved, now cold and lifeless. One could not breathe life into it, no matter how many sighs escaped one's lips. The warm tears falling onto those lips could not make them quiver. No, those lips would not voice words now, for death could *not* be reversed. Why did one keep bending one's head, straining one's ears in the hope of catching a barely perceptible rhythm, a missed heartbeat, perhaps? Would a tiny drop of blood trickle into those secret chambers, through those thin, veiled, thinly veiled, translucent cusps and somehow urge the heart to squeeze even those last droplets of pain out? *Just that much and no more?* It was just a matter of one last contraction, one rapid upstroke and then even the heart could rest.

There was still some time left, before the hands of the clock would coincide, before one big veined hand would eclipse the other smaller one. Before his slender, delicate fingers would touch her shorter, stouter ones...

She didn't know why her heart hurt so much. It just *did*. It seemed as if it had known nothing else, as if this had become its natural state. It's *only* state...

There was still time. Still time to learn. The hands hadn't yet melted in each other's arms. There was still some time left, she reminded herself.

She picked up her pen and scribbled in her journal....

You know what I long for?

I long for spring

Spring in my heart

Spring in my soul

Spring in my body

I long for a lush carpet of grass

under my bare feet

soft, moist, tender

I long for shadows to meet

blend, mix, shrink

and finally vanish

Don't you wish that too?

I wish for tranquil silences within to grow

'Fiddle' with my strings, will you?

Will you?

I want to tip toe over the planks

and dip my heel in the snow

I want snow, I want spring

I want snow to 'fall' in spring

Will I be given this birthday gift?

All worlds in one?

Nay! Just the eye to see

Will I be granted that, I ask thee?

Just this once

Please God,

I know I have been acting rather odd

Just this once?

Just this once?

Regret was a lethal poison, a slow acting one at that. It kept her gripped in the clutches of the past. It spread slowly in her veins, turning her skin blue, making her mouth froth near the corners, until she was completely paralyzed--caught tightly in the claws of what could have been, but wasn't. A perennial locked-in state. That's where it imprisoned her. She could breathe, move her eyes this way and that, but her gaze kept returning to the landscape from the past. What plagued her was her immaculate ability to romanticize the past. That's how history was seriously flawed. It depended entirely on who was writing it and from what vantage point. Her right could very well, then become that which was left. While what was left was just never right for him. And thus, they bickered and argued tirelessly.

Longing, a frequent accompaniment of regret, made the dull grey picture even more sombre. To long for what was left behind was not right. No, it couldn't possibly be, for it only fossilized her hopelessly.... Yes, she knew all this so well. She had helped innumerable travelers with this pearl of wisdom, yet here she was caught in the cobwebs of her own creating. Her own 'figment of imagination,' she scoffed.

Regret.... Longing...

She longed for a day when she would have no regrets.

For now, she longed for nothing else but a peaceful night. If sleep entwined her arms around her tense body, she would feel no regret. None whatsoever.

To be caught in a whirlpool of longings?

A long, winding staircase leading up to nowhere?

Unsung songs, untold stories

Breaths that never mingled

Heads that never found shoulders to cry on.

Journeys never embarked upon

Destinations never reached.

Trees dried up of all sap

Branches that never bore fruits

Roots that could never be *truly* displaced

Wings that were never spread out

Sunrises missed by her sleepy, dreamy eyes

Sunsets that sank her burdened heart.

Thoughts that floated, light as a feather

blending with the vast, vast grey skies.

Words not spoken, never reaching her ears

Poetry not making its way into hearts--

Clamped. Clogged. Closed. Cloistered.

Just brushing past ears, a momentary light touch

Those tiny droplets trickling down, feebly

Distilling from her soul, drop by drop by drop

carried away, lost in the ocean, insignificant, forgotten

Once cast into a firm, steady mould

congealed and solidified.

Now *abandoned, deserted.*

left searching for new meanings

Bewildered children, motherless, orphaned

tiny innocent fingers tugging on strangers' hands

pale, masked faces searching for forgotten smiles

peals of laughter sought in cold, deep sighs

A whirlpool of longings waiting to be fulfilled…

The only way to deal with fear was by facing it, she was told. The only way to live life was by living. Not running. Not hiding. Because there was no escape. And probably after the initial ordeal was over, it wouldn't seem so difficult after all.

She kept holding onto this flimsy curtain, hiding behind it and closing her eyes, hoping since she couldn't see the world, so would the world be oblivious of her.

What did she want? To become invisible for a few hours? Isn't that what she had been craving for? To don the invisibility cloak and forget she belonged here. Forget she was part of all this. Forget herself. Forget the world. Forget it all. Just dive inside her mind's eye. And sleep like an embryo there.

But she wasn't an embryo anymore. She no longer was that little girl that would sit on her father's scooter with her face facing backwards, just for the thrill of moving against the tide. She remembered how her tiny hand clutched onto that black tyre. And here she was now. Clutching onto dear life. And yet not really living. 'Stop holding it so tightly! she admonished herself. 'Let it take you. Flow and melt in her arms. Blend with it. Let those colors dissolve all your shades. Internalize that music. Synchronize your breathing with it, let your heart match that pace.'

'Be water. Be vapor. Be ice. Assume all forms. Glide from one to the other effortlessly. Let the sky meet the earth. Be like the crack of dawn. That fraction of a second when night is consumed by the first hint of light. Freeze that moment. Stretch it to an eternity. These two extremes could blend. They always can. And when they do, they do so beautifully, imperceptibly, gracefully. Remember that mighty chinar? Remember how it carries all shades in those carefully carved out leaves? The green of spring and summer, the gold and brown of autumn and the crimson and vague gray of the winter ahead. What colour is yours? Pray! Come now!

Don't let the greys overshadow your other hues. What a waste that would be! The beauty lies in the entire gamut. The whole palette. Don't be a dull, dreary painting, she reminded herself, when there is the possibility of being a colourful delight. Mix all your colours well. See how just a tiny drop from your brush colours the water of your soul. Watch it dissolve. Slowly...You think sunshine and rain cannot coexist? Have you forgotten the joy of spotting a rainbow as a child? Remember how those tiny drops of rain suspended in air would act like tiny prisms, breaking the rays of the sun? One colourful arc embracing another? The seven heavens painted brilliantly.

If water can do it, if the trees can do it, so can the skies and the rainbow arching across it, what makes you think you can't?'

She tilts her tired little head and writes on the mirror.

I am water

I am vapor

I am ice too

I am the green of summer

The gold of autumn

And the winter grey too

I am the seven colours of broken white

And the unsplit white too

I am rain and sun juxtaposed

I am night being devoured by the crack of dawn

That first flash of light piercing through the darkness

The bow, the arrow and the archer too

I am both putrid and fragrant

I am a jumbled mix of words

A random pick of musical notes

He will make poetry out of it

He will let the songs flow

How? You think I know?

Just hang in there

He will show...

She had to learn to breathe again, to crawl and drag herself and then slowly, but steadily get up on her feet and learn how to walk all over again, tiny baby steps, one at a time. How indomitable and daunting it seemed now! What a Herculean task set out for her! From delighting in silences to suddenly fearing it, she had come a full circle. Just in one moment. One infinitesimally small fraction was all it had taken. One sudden spiraling down, one enormous descent into the deepest depths of the void, one sudden snap of a finger. She could barely make head or tail (or even a tantalizing tale!) of what drove her to a point of such absolute disconnect with the world around her and the world within her. All she knew was that she had curled inwards, like a bud refusing to blossom, a flower wilting and withering, a child forcing his eyes shut, an embryo refusing birth. To *be here* and *yet not*, was something she could barely explain, to even her own self, let alone to others!

"How could I become so defeatist!" she sighed in exasperation.

Yes, she felt a tug -two worlds, two contrasts, pulling at her in diagonally opposite directions. She could feel the chill of winter and the oppressive heat of the sultry sun, both. *Simultaneously* and *acutely*. And to find one's balance amid this seasonal storm was easier said than done. One had to realign one's inner compass, reset one's thermostat at *just* the right temperature. It was a tiring ordeal. A painful, tormenting one at that! To attempt a laugh when one saw very little humor in life? And to dance when no music could reach one's heart? *What* could be harder than that?

Her shoulders had begun drooping under the tremendous weight they toted. That of a swollen, empty head-overinflated, hydrocephalic, she thought to herself with a hint of a smile tickling the corner of her mouth, tip toeing sneakily, unexpectedly, like a vaguely familiar acquaintance calling upon her unannounced, catching her off-guard. Her mouth had been stretched into a straight line for months now, slit like, an orifice that gave away very little, except for dropping hints of sadness, now and then. There was too much 'water' in that goddamn head of hers and the pressure that kept building within, burst open the tightly guarded floodgates when she least expected it and then there was no stopping the sudden cascade that roared forth!

She, somehow, needed to be more porous now, more permeable. So, this river could flow in and out of her, unobstructed, unencumbered, freely finding its way. She could barely withstand another deluge, she repeated to herself. It submerged her completely, her head struggling to rise above the water, gasping for air, limbs flapping in all possible directions. And sadly, it inundated everything else around her too. This tornado had the cataclysmic potential of destroying everything and everyone that came in its path. And the wreckage of that wrath terrified her terribly.

So, she would write and write and write, until her eyes too would turn blind...

She wrote agitatedly, angrily, in a mad frenzy, as if her *very existence* depended upon it. Vague, incoherent string of thoughts kept hitting her head, flitting across speedily, a jumbled, muddled, muddied haze-meaningless gibberish to most, including her on 'saner' days. Yet this was to be her *only respite*, her *elixir.* She was to take this medicine ritually as advised, flush it down her throat swiftly, in one rapid gulp, a hint of bitter, metallic aftertaste lingering on her tongue, long after. It was no quick-fix, she had been warned. She had no choice but to be patient, to bear with the caustic, corrosive acidity of her prescribed medication, the accompanying heart-burn. It would work its way slowly into her heart (once adequately burnt), her physician had assured her and bring her back from the dead. That would be the course of her slow revival, no matter how protracted it seemed.

It was *this* resurrection that she awaited. *A Renaissance of her soul...Again...*

A gust that would finally reach her dull black hair and whisper gently, but clearly enough, into the convolutions of her delicately carved out, tiny ears "Spring will be here soon, and the nightingale will sing songs of love and hope, and you will spring back to life, again…. Yet again…."

For the hope of a rise lay but, in the fall...

Dear Sun,

Tonight, I feel a shroud of sadness engulf me from all sides. Don't ask me why. I will open my heart to you. Slowly but surely. You must be patient, darling, as must I. Even though my heart is bogged down under the tremendous weight it carries, I felt terribly light. Light as a feather. You know why? Because I had finally let go of my ego. That unnecessary baggage that I toted around. I didn't need it anymore. I was being cooked gently on this flame and I could not help but be grateful to Him.

I needed to die, I told Death

Come, come take me in your arms

Embrace me, kiss my cold lips

Suck my soul out of the confines

Of narrow lanes, those tall brick walls

I supplicate, I beseech, listen, pay heed

Hug me, Death, the way I need...

You are my wheel

The spoke that spoke to me

Before I diverged from the hub

Those iron rods still pierced my heart

As my distance from my zero increased

Come, come, hold my trembling hands now

Come, come, take the lead

Tilled I wait, come, plant your seed

Drill those holes in my soul

Take me to your lips, play me as a reed

Blow your breath into my being

Your music, your notes, your air

Torn pages flying by, here

Inked and forgotten, no eyes to read

Come, Death, come, dance

A dance, with me, sway

Sway, sway, into that land

Take me by the hand

Let all those grains slip by now

All time, those moments, stolen and how

Let the waves wash over this sand...

Come, come, take me by the hand...

You know Sun, when you give someone the weapon to destroy you and still believe with all your heart that they won't and there you see the dagger being plunged right into your heart, you feel no pain. Absolutely none. Instead, you smile peacefully. You smile as you see how your own love had the power to transform. No one else but your own heart. If it doesn't soften your coarseness, if it doesn't smoothen your callosities, what good was it to you in the first place? Dear, if you sense anguish in my missive, be dismissive of it. Pain, yearning, longing, pathos no longer touches me where I am. No, I haven't hardened, my love. In fact, so crushed and softened am I that all those elements have mixed completely with the earth. He kneaded the dough so well, that no lump remains anymore. I am grateful for this. I am grateful for the lightning that struck my forehead. I had flung my hands wide open, I had waited with bated breath for the gust to tear me apart. You think I mourn? You see me bending down on my knees. You assume I bend down to gather the tattered shreds of my existence? You couldn't be farther from the truth. I bend down in humility. In submission. In gratitude. Ripped off thus, I am given a new lease of life. What is pain, Sun? Why do we suffer? Why must I carry the cross on my back? Why must those nails rend my skin, lacerate my ego, fracture my stiff backbone? You think pain is but in vain? What is in it that we truly gain? Yes, my kindred soul, resurrection is an attainable goal. If you see my body stiffen, my hands struggle, my breath reaches my lips, do not clutch your heart. Don't shield it. I'm not dying. I'm being born yet again. Yet another life in this life, can you see the beauty of it? I'm so happy being turned to dust. So happy to mix with the soil beneath those feet.

Tread softly now, or march at maddening speed, I care not.

I am dust.

And I must fly.

Off your feet

Into the sky....

My love

Renewed, reborn

S.

We shall meet again

And the stars shall fall in my lap

and the grass shall grow on that barren land

a self-perpetuating, prolific carpet of green

A rebirth after the first shower of rain

We shall then, meet again...

When my trembling knees would regain their strength

and the laughter of loved ones would resonate within

When the creases around eyes would smoothen and ease

and hearts thawed, brought back to life, shall never freeze

When there shall be no shadow of the shadow of that pain

We shall then, meet again...

When the kindness of hearts would melt all snow

and streams of poetry would innately flow

untouched, unheard, unblemished, unseen

When the origin and end shall finally meet

That heaven shall *then* be under her feet

When all the thorns of torment would have been plucked away

and new seeds of hope planted along the way.

All tears would have been gathered when

white water lilies would soak them in

minute droplets, breaking and coalescing

That's when the heart shall follow this undertaking

We shall then, meet again...

when music shall flow from my empty silence

and my heart shall mirror my own true self

When the sun shall shine in its reclaimed light

and the reflected glow of the moon shall wane

It is then, that we shall meet again....

The task set out for her was simple. She had to sift out the 'right' grains of sand from the 'wrong' ones. In her heart and in her mind. All the cards were carefully laid out on the wide table before her. A daunting, staggering pile stared her in the face. The 'blacks' needed to be grabbed by their necks and spaded out from the 'reds'. One strong decisive blow was all that was required of her. One crush, one definitive stomp. It seemed all very easy, pragmatically speaking, only that pragmatism failed terribly as a strategy, in the ineffable plane. Her Garden of Eden had been converted into a cemetery in one fleeting moment and that burial ground bore a lone, solitary tombstone. Flowers had been trampled, the soil had been soiled, tiny tender bulbs had been twisted and wrenched out treacherously.

Her soul too was besmirched, muddied, stained and sullied. While her body died, the soul thrived; rising all the way up the grey, leaden skies, her soul still fragrant and strong. Purple, delicate hyacinths encircled the ripples created on the surface of the seemingly serene, limpid waters. Vapors wafted upwards from mundane little conversations; their worlds meeting in tiny teacups, stirred effortlessly, reaching the very pinnacle of sharp, jagged snow-peaks on the one hand, and the deepest depths of the frothy oceans on the other. Their worlds had intermingled inextricably, danced deliriously and jingled joyously with each other. And then, it had all poured down in one torrential storm. Or was it a gentle trickle? How her traitorous heart had tricked her!

"Was it a gentle trickle? "

She bit her tongue-as tiny drops coalesced in the soft feathery clouds above-brimming till the very brink, overflowing slowly, drop by drop-percolating the parched soil of their souls, now fully soaked. It kept seeping deeper and deeper down, reaching her very core that was all at once hot and ready to erupt. To wipe that deluge out required far more than a fancy whim. Bits of her soul, that she had carefully spread out like a carpet beneath those uncaring feet, had to be retrieved. Her halves sprinkled amidst the pages of a long-forgotten book had to be gathered back too. That book lay untouched now, the pages had turned yellow, fading, having been burnt in the sunny evenings of shared intimacy-- a laugh here, a sigh there, excited exclamations, sudden, euphoric gasps. Those pages were dull and grey now, forlorn for a revisit, a random gaze from an old fellow traveler.

She kept coming back, combing, rummaging, raking through those lines, looking for parts she had hopelessly left behind. *Unknowingly, naively.* Her stories had impossibly, irretrievably been mixed with the tales carried inside those pages. A poignantly beautiful, a painfully tragic, an intricately woven, delicate *pashmina* shawl lay unattended now, being blown away in the gentle breeze. "Sad little murder of innocence, and in *blinding* broad daylight too!" she muttered through her pursed, parched lips.

She dashed out suddenly, lunging forward in one desperate, last ditch act of self-preservation. *One ultimate act of self-annihilation.*

"Frozen feelings in frozen hearts had to be pecked at repeatedly with an old rusty mallet," she reminded herself. The chipped off, sharp shards of ice kept burying underneath, deeper and deeper in her heart, with every little nudge. She kept inhaling warm air rapidly, hungrily, expanding her chest, making way for some more air. And some more pain. She knew she had to *hold, withhold* and *contain* all this and much more. She had to amalgamate both the freezing coldness of ice and the scorching heat of fire. What could *possibly* be created by such an alchemical reaction, she knew not. But she made insane attempts at preserving *both* in their natural, elemental forms--*ice and fire, fire and ice,* caught in endless throes *with* each other, *for* each other and ultimately *against* each other--one annulling the other, one mirroring the other too, offsetting, contradicting, conflicting, but eventually forgetting their individual quirks and blending, fusing, comingling, coexisting.

She had set out on a path seeking truth, her *own* version of it. She had wandered, gone astray. She had been lost in the woods, having come so close to *one* tree that she had lost all sight of the forest. And *now* she had forgotten whatever she had been seeking, forgotten whatever she had chanced upon. She had *even* forgotten that she had forgotten. She no longer knew what oblivion looked like and so she had to start all over again, she had to *re-seek* with a new pair of eyes and a renewed vision.

Each time she attempted to set herself free, her frivolous, playful hand would get caught repeatedly in that huge Wheel of Time. She twisted, contorted and bled profusely. She *did* manage to free herself in the end, but one persistent sore clamped her down, choked her and clipped her wings; one tiny circle that she had drawn around herself, with her *then* flippant hands was to enclose her forever. Fossilized and ossified, she was thus caught in a time warp, between *here* and *there*. "What a trap this one proved to be in the end!" she exhaled in exasperation. No cozy, comforting wrap was draped around her shivering shoulders on cold, dry wintery nights, no embers burnt, no light seeped into her soul here.

All the doors and windows of that suffocating, bleak cage had been fiercely shut upon her, yet shadowed voices kept reverberating in her feverish head. She felt she could hear bullets being fired into the air, pellets penetrating eyeballs, and one long poignant wail piercing the darkness of these black nights. The sounds that kept striking, resonating and echoing within her, emanated all but from a singular source. It was pumped forth from her *own* heart, coursed through her veins, hooking and entangling her raw nerves on its way, journeying up through her crazy, stubborn head- "Silly figments of my imagination!" she mocked herself.

Brick by brick by brick she dismantled the image of that 'home' in her head, only to find her heart aching unbearably, buried under the crushing weight of that immense rubble. She kept hammering at the monumental ruin with renewed fervor, a ritual performed with the utmost care, slow and deliberate at first, a pause to catch her breath. She stopped just as abruptly as she had begun the whole tormenting exercise. She suddenly burst into a flurry of tears and kept staring at her coarse, empty hands. She cast one glance upon her heart, and another one over her shoulders, gazing distantly at all that she had left far behind. *A long, blank and empty look.*

She went back to work, deliriously pulling out all monsters from her memory, one exacting, entangled weed at a time.

One garment torn, flung and thrown away

Another apparel donned.

One exile imposed

Yet another pilgrimage undertaken.

And one long, long road ahead...

Delhi was shrouded in a thick blanket of grey smoke- pungent, suffocating, asphyxiating. This horrible cloak was choking her too. Those dull, dreary, bleak and heavy skies had the menacing power of dragging one's soul down with its oppressive weight. Such heaviness she felt! In the air outside and that which reached her insides. There was something so sinister about it, so hugely powerful. It made you pale into insignificance, a tiny little dot, powerless and obscure. This desolation and gloom could creep into your house, just float in quietly from any door or window, no matter how tightly clamped. It just knew its way in. So sure, and authoritative it was, no less than a phantom, a ghost of memories, of lost longing. Wisps of smoky dark apparitions kept colliding, drifting, gliding and hovering over her heart until they sank--*both* smoke and heart. This black cloud shrouded her completely today.

She inhaled deeply, with all her might, fearing not what muck went inside her, forcing her clogged lungs to open and then, with more of desperation than force that she could summon, tried to exhale and blow that cloud away. No easy games these were. It wasn't like she had, fancifully, decided to snuff out a candle, it's light already dim, it's flame flickering, already breathing it's last, with tiny molten beads of wax, reminiscent of hours of burning, having already rolled down, reaching the very base, the few moments before the final extinction. Poof! Gone! And darkness. How easy would that be!

This, however, was far more excruciating. It was like a full blown, raging fire that had to be doused out and modest bucketsful of brine tears (even those drying up now) were no match for such a conflagration. *Why not,* you ask? This inferno, my friend, was no ordinary one. It would start very innocently, spread wildly, at lightning speed and engulf in its wrath your most vulnerable, your most valuable, also your weakest, your softest, *that* which you had deluded yourself into believing was safely kept away, hidden from the line of fire, locked up in the safest of 'chests', she smiled.

And see now? A tiny matchstick carelessly thrown into an inflammable, volatile mind was all it had taken. A *volatile* mind from a *volatile* valley, she barely voiced those words, and before you could steady yourself, regain your balance and scratch your head to begin to fathom what hit you, it was already too late. Mind ablaze, ignited, delirious, the fire spreading far and wide, turning to ash anything that crossed its agitated, frenzied, feverish madness.

Fire. Smoke. And saline tears.

Imagine the perilous, fatal concoction that was brewing inside of her. Crackling insanity! She cackled.

Yet, she stirred and stirred and stirred relentlessly, hoping for the fire to dim, the smoke to settle down and the salt to either evaporate into 'nothingness' or dissolve completely into the immense ocean of her 'being.' *Now. Forever*

"Creativity and fidelity could not coexist," he had remarked half seriously, half-jokingly. She remembered that afternoon so well. Returning from work, she had just reached home and had lingered on at the gate longer than usual. She could almost feel the touch of the cold metallic knob against her skin again, as she had lifted it up that day, to let herself in. She had abruptly ended that conversation, like so many conversations that had been left unfinished, hanging in mid-air. Words that were still being strung together in the head, thoughts that were still being gathered neatly like fresh white lilies plucked from the garden, still lying in that basket waiting to be threaded into a garland. It was so strange. Of the million things that she could choose from, this somehow had solidified in her memory. And now it had caught her completely off guard. Leaping out of some tightly shut drawer, it had pounced upon her and settled somewhere in her numbed mind. Suddenly, that beast in hibernation, had chosen this unearthly hour to stretch its massive body, shake and awaken from its slumber.

Creativity, by its innate nature, was averse to fidelity, she was told. One negated the other. You could either be faithful and hopelessly unimaginative or vacillating, perfidious, fickle and brilliantly original. To be Promethean thus, required you to be promiscuous. Intellectually, at least, if not otherwise. And in this daring, original, heroic act of stirring passions, fire needn't be stolen from Zeus for the greater good of humanity. No Pandora would be sent to Earth to charm the wits off creative geniuses in the offing. And hence, Prometheus would suffer no curse. No bits of his liver would be eaten off by eagles, only to be regenerated in the night, to relive this eternal punishment repeatedly. No. This argument couldn't possibly hold ground. Not for her, at least. Her insides (her own liver, the whole of it!) were churning to say otherwise. Creativity, like fidelity, required a careful nibbling away from the mind, the soul, from one's very core. And for those flashes of supposed 'inspirations', did one need a battalion of borrowed, hired 'soldiers' to fight one's wars? One would wager not. Too tired to delve any deeper, she walked up those flight of stairs, took a deep breath and turned the handle of another door leading into another 'home'....

99

She picks up a twig and draws on the wet sand,

awash with waves

Her hands move slowly to inscribe two lines,

running parallel to each other...

two worlds, moving away in opposite directions

One reality negating and belying the other,

fading and receding far, far away

She closes her eyes and lets her mind wander

in the lanes and by lanes of home

seeking refuge on this path of exile....

They say, the dried *Chinar* leaves have long been burnt

heaps after heaps after heaps of memories

Their crispness has long been crushed, they say

The colors of autumn have faded long, long ago

that crimson and rust and orange and gold

Even the smoke emanates from those burnt leaves no more.

They say, my lake has frozen now,

frozen into untouched, unbroken stillness

and voices have been trapped beneath that ice

not finding a way to break through the barrier,

now solid and cold.

They say, one can no longer even see ones' reflection in it

for weeds and algae have grown exuberantly

in those untended regions

spreading like a green carpet ensheathing frozen hearts...

They say, skies are heavy and overcast now

and ghosts with sunken eyes walk in the nights

dressed in dull grey *pherans*, their shoulders droop

under the weight of the gloomy, grey skies

under the weight of those chiseled mountains

now covered with snow.

Folklores have frozen too, they say

The winds carrying them got tired on the way.

Glaciers of sadness have been left behind,

where joyous streams once flowed, they say

waiting for the sun to come out of the dark clouds

and melt the frozen, unshed tears away...

They say, your heart is heavy too

for you carry home in exile with you

and the burden will lighten in a while

once you are at home in this exile...

Back home in Kashmir, it was snowing again. It *had*, in fact, been snowing for the past many days, she had heard. She felt betrayed, *utterly* betrayed. Back stabbed. *How* could it have snowed so much? How could it have snowed *at all*? When she was so far away? How many miles stretched between her home and her heart? She felt a pang of jealousy creep slowly into her bosom. Even words reaching her end would be frozen no more. She held the phone close to her ears so that she could, somehow magically, feel that freezing chilly wind tickle her earlobes. But Delhi was so far, she sighed. So *very* far. Even the icy words would melt on their way here, being suspended in midair for too long. And those tiny trickles that *did* manage to reach her lips could hardly quench her thirst.

Delhi was so far.... So far....

Her mind wandered again. Memories. Darn them! Guileful, crafty, artful. She marveled at her helplessness at the hands of her own memories. They would lead her on deftly, subtly--at times leaving behind no more than a faint earthy smell, a whiff off her silken body--and *in* she dived, in a state of complete hypnosis. That devious nymph took her on journeys in those snow-clad mountains, inside the lush green forests of her own heart. She closed her eyes and simply followed, no questions asked, no answers sought, no knowledge of the path, no hope of reaching any destination. She simply let herself be carried away, caressing them, fondling them, being caressed and fondled back too, losing herself to them completely, with total surrender, complete abandon. She would go wherever the winds would take her...

Delhi was so far...Now

While once she had thought...

'Delhi is not far'....

She remembered the slim book bearing that title from ages ago. Was it this lifetime even? Another world perhaps? The picture on the jacket of the book, sepia or perhaps grey--of two men riding a bicycle in the shade of a

103

tree (which she now imagined to be the *Chinar*) --would have grayed further, awaiting her return, resting in some corner of her carpeted room. Whether she read it or not, she could hardly recall now. But the mere memory of that book evoked a deep sense of longing in her heart tonight. She had known it all along. That *this* would be her story. Dreaming dreams of leaving the nest, but never really *wanting* to, hoping to possess, but never really desiring ownership. There was an element of kinship, an inexplicable closeness that she had felt with that novella. A bond shared beyond the words of Bond, she smiled. So, while she foolishly imagined 'life being elsewhere', she knew in her heart, all along, that life was nowhere else, but *there*. In her 'home.' And now only in her heart. For she was to carry 'home' wherever she went, on her shoulders, in the creases of her palms, in the delicate gold brushstrokes of her tiny papier-mache jewelry box, in the comforting warmth of her emerald *pashmina* shawl that snuggled around her neck, in the delicate white snowflakes trapped, forever, in the black net of her moist eyelashes...

The snowflakes were still falling there, as she wiped her eyelashes here. She hardly needed to close her eyes to conjure up that picture. It had formed the landscape of her heart all along, after all. That skyline, those jagged mountains, sculpted and chiseled to perfection. She knew it all so well, like the back of her hand.

The eerie stillness, that unbroken silence lay draped in white tonight, the pristine white of snow, to blot out all the blackness...And wash away all the red poured onto the streets in the summer....

And as it rained here in Delhi, so many miles away, it carried the faintly familiar, distant smell of snow admixed with it...

She let that curtain of snow fall on her drooping eyelids, snow interlaced and woven intricately with all her dreams, the ones she had dreamt of and forgotten, as also the ones she was yet to dream...

This winter there would be no winter. Not even a pale shadow of what winter truly was for her. No freezing heads carrying frozen thoughts, tucked beneath layers and layers of quilts, no cold feet, frostbitten, cyanosed, no fog escaping lips as they speak, those ghosts of words mingling mid-air, vapors colliding, losing all form, fusing with the words exhaled by a friend, words thus breathed in and breathed out rhythmically, cold, chilly words inhaled and warmed inside ones heart.

No smoke would escape those tall blackened chimneys

No water running through metallic pipes would freeze,

those serpents refusing to slither or hiss.

No bare trees would be seen this time.

the skeletons remaining once the flesh had fallen off

those naked, wiry branches spreading, sprawling no more.

No feet shall be warmed, thawed back to life

over the hearth beneath which embers lay

Dried stumps and branches of trees dried up

now burn as dead logs of wood…in the *hamam*

The mountains shall play hide-and-seek with her no more

hidden from sight as the blanket of fog comes to the fore...

Reappearing suddenly when draped in white curtains of snow…

Snow, you say? Yes… Snow

Has it fallen yet or are the skies still heavy and grey?

Who would tell me now? How would I know?

Who would pull apart those curtains each morning

to see if sleepy eyes would awaken from one dream to another?

with squinting eyes, half closed, half open

who would see that magical white carpet

spread delicately in the garden below?

The branches of trees no longer bare

bearing down under the weight of snow.

Each twig, each curve sensuously traced

touched, blanketed in a lover's embrace.

Whose feet would be happy to feel the crunching sound

when they would touch that white ground

But this winter shall bring no snow

No freezing sighs

No heavy skies

No gloom too, you say?

But wait! First let this one allay…

Alas! This winter there shall be no winter…

Chapter 3

Clunk!

So here it was. Staring her right in the face. And there was no way that she could escape the ineluctability of it, whether she liked it or not, whether she had asked for it or not--*Life was more powerful than death*. It had won tonight. There was no other way to it. Death would win one day. Life would finally give herself up, wholly, body and soul, into the arms of that damned lover, the scoundrel that had jilted her this time. But that would be some other night filled with passion. Tonight, she simply bowed her head down to Life. Tonight, she nestled up in those tender arms, being rocked gently in that cradle.

"How could I have driven myself to this point again!" she thought through bitter tears of frustration. Just *how!* How could you have reached the same crossroads having already crossed that bridge! How could one revert to the point from where one had once started, so many years ago? She had moved backwards. Yes, that's what it was. And with no sight to lead her on, she was bound to fall. As she had, on many occasions before. As she did, once again. Her refusal to want to live made him livid, for no other reason, but because he saw death up, close and front, every single moment, each hour that he was awake, revisiting it in the nights as well. What he essentially did, was to help people race against time, stealing a few months for some on good days and mere seconds for others, on a bad one. He bargained with death, conned and duped her. She was an 'interpreter of maladies,' while he, the healer.

And so, her desire to give it all up, infuriated him beyond imagination. He took it *too* personally, he was livid with rage, kept glowering at her incessantly, his entire body shaking like a massive tree, until her trembling hand steadied itself and the cold metallic knife she had held in it, slipped through her fingers. As she heard the clunking sound of the metal striking against the marble floor, the reality of what she was doing suddenly hit her and she felt her stomach contract horribly. She felt sick, *nauseatingly* sick! She dashed to the bathroom to vomit out all that had been poisoning her. She retched all that bilious rage out.

Clunk!

That sharp, shrill, brief sound reverberated in her mind as she tried to sleep.

Clunk!

With that, she dropped the thought of ending her life. She had not created it, she had no right to destroy it either.

"What you don't create will end up destroying you"...

His words had been prophetic, as if he could gaze inside her soul with his penetrating sight.

Closing her eyes, she tried her best to recall where and how it all started. Was it in the sweet, earthy smell of damp soil after the first showers? Those vapors of steam rising from the moist soil that had been roasting in the sultry sun, aching with longing for those cool drops to quench her thirst, or was it the giddiness she had felt, that queer pleasurable, nervous excitement, anticipating the first snowfall, reading the skies, hearing the blaring sirens in that silence? She was no seer, her hands held no crystal ball to gaze into, there were no leaves left in her cup of tea as she drank it, swallowing the whole thing down in one gulp, no patterns were made for her to read from, and in any case, she was unlettered. Who could have predicted such a dark, bleak future and yet laugh carelessly, without a worry in the world? Suddenly, all her past, present and future had been blended, merged and painted with a single, sweeping stroke of black. This is how the dark ghosts of the past could cast looming shadows on all that was yet to come. This is what the wise had warned them against. But even *then*, they had been blind. Blind and deaf...

They had eyes yet couldn't see. And now, even those eyes were being gouged out, one by one by one, scooped out like a dollop of red currant ice cream, cold and bloodied.

They had all been blind, including her. What was worse was that she possessed an overly overworked head and that's where all her unease seemed to stem from. From the rocky, mountainous terrain of her heart too, perhaps. Yes, that's what it was. It hadn't suddenly dawned upon her one fine morning. No, this was no epiphany, no brilliant flash of lightning that had struck her suddenly, taking her minute body in its massive grip and shaking her up. This process had been slow, painfully slow and it was trying to tell her something, trying to take her somewhere, forcing her to unlearn all that she thought she had learnt, to make way for some new lessons to be learnt, in *this* life.

The stillness of the room only compounded its darkness. She lay her head softly on the pillow allowing sleep to take her away from herself... Far away...Into the realm of the unknown...

This was the lull *after* the storm.... And she was still recovering from the cataclysm of the night before....

"Go gentle on my heart, O tempest," she whispered quietly...

She waited in the car for his return. Her gaze wandered about aimlessly, until it was transfixed upon the pool of water sprawling before her. From one quaint, spicular fountain sprung forth tiny hillocks of froth. The water seemed to be on the boil, stoked by some invisible fire underneath, bubbling over, rising, until it descended and joined the common pool. It seemed edgy, troubled and unquiet, just like her. She kept staring at the upward movement of the jet, at the dancing, leaping mounts, and the trembling, shaky drops as they gushed down. The windows of the car were pulled up, but she could almost hear the gurgling sound in her head.

Splish...Splash...Splish...Splash...

She closed her eyes, as if transitioning from one dream to another.

Everything seemed the same. The tilting rays of the sun casting oblong, elongated shadows on the sparkling, transparent surface of water. The same azure skies above and the same her. *Yet...Yet*, there were no fountains spurting mouthfuls of foaming fluid here and no massive ripples were created, except the ones formed around that *heart* shaped oar, as it split the river in two, with the red and yellow paint of the oar having nearly peeled off until it was barely visible. She could now smell that unique, pure, unsullied smell of wet deodar. Not just *any* smell she thought. The smell of Jhelum seeping into Deodar...The faint whiff of the beloved left on the arms of the lover, long after their night of union. This was that sweet amalgamation of permanence with transience--the hardness and the solidity of that wood seasoned in the fluidity of water--that meeting point of unlikely friends, of strangers thrown onto each other's path by some random chance and then, journeying together, marching ahead on a pilgrimage. A pilgrimage into the unknown, a peregrination into the interior of one's own heart, a mad, reckless, impetuous plunge into each other's too. And there she was, holding onto hers, clasping it in a tight self-embrace, being ferried across the Jhelum in a water gondola...in her little boat...her *shikara*...

Everything seemed the same. Her, the sun, the river. Even the *shikara wala* had seemed vaguely familiar. His lopsided grin had bedazzled her. It was contagious. She found her lips stretch beyond her volition and the corners turn upwards into a soft, sad smile. For though everything seemed the same, even the little eddies formed on the surface, yet nothing truly was like before. Just when she had reached the middle of the river, with one bank receding far behind and the opposite bank appearing in sight, it suddenly struck her.

Where was home now?

That which she had left behind,

or that which lay ahead?

"There is no home here for you. Nothing of the sort exists, not for you, not for anyone. Don't delude yourself, don't be such a fool!" Her father's voice had been crisp and clear that evening. He had very succinctly explained the real meaning of life and death to her; of impermanence and transience. Concise, pithy, crystal clear. Just like the water before her eyes.

The only truth was this...That all this, the *here* and the *now,* was a lie and the truth, lay hidden somewhere within the folds of this lie. We know it all along, yet, somewhere, somehow, we managed to forget, for we *must* forget, we *need* to forget to make it from one day to the other.

She recalled the look of detachment in her grandfather's eyes, as they sat down on the verandah that opened onto their lush green garden. He had sounded so distant, so removed as he had spoken to her in whispered tones. "I couldn't sleep the whole night, I was flipping through some old black and white pictures." She had felt a pang of inexplicable sadness that evening. How well she remembered it! Nostalgia was a poison that had the potential of paralyzing its victims. It could immobilize them, fossilizing and trapping them forever in an ice slab of the past. It was a crippling, incapacitating, debilitating disease. And how they *all* suffered from it!

They had all wanted to relive their past, in one way or the other....

"I feel like I am split into halves."

Her uncle had nearly choked on his own words. She remembered that dull, gloomy evening in winter, when he had tentatively begun opening his wounds before swiftly covering them up again. The living room was dimly lit, warm and cozy, yet his heart had shivered from the cold within. She couldn't really understand the nature of that pain or the import those words carried in a deeper, more profound way, but she had felt a sudden tug on her heart. Yes, he had managed to run away, run away from the mess that his childhood had been, run away from all the strife, the conflict that had surrounded him, but his escape had only been spatial. Some ghosts managed to run faster than we possibly could and sooner or later caught up with us, crossing all boundaries, all barriers of culture, continents, time zones, transcending all impediments of age, experience, reality or duality. Some wounds were unrelenting, refusing time as a healer. Unattended, ignored, they only expanded, aggravated, growing multitudinously until they ruptured, gave way, dehisced and then we would have an acute emergency on our hands.

He must have been in his late fifties then, gray haired with a slightly protruding belly, like most men his age. His face bore a striking resemblance with his mother's, the same blunt nose, that was high bridged no doubt, but somewhere along the way had been abruptly rounded off, as if someone was beginning to start off on a high-pitched note but was curtly cut off in mid-sentence. His mouth was the same as well, deep nasolabial folds that seemed carefully carved out. A scowl would require very little effort for such a face, not that she recollected him scowling very often. But then again, she barely saw him more than once a year and that too, for a few months in summer, so she couldn't say much about how that face might have danced to various emotions. The only thing that she *did* know, however, was that he kept himself extremely busy, always dashing in and

113

out of countries, spending much of his time suspended in air. He barely slept, she was told, jet lag being no deterrent to him. He was all of nineteen when he had run away from home and he kept running at breakneck speed.

But running *towards* what? Running *away* from whom?

Many years later, his native land, his *Kasheer*, was to witness an exodus of sort with young boys, many far younger than him, running away from their homes too, but to *what* end?

And then, we had another tragic exodus too.

Of homes being abandoned in the dead of the night, not even the skeletons remained there now.

"We tend to reproduce the extrinsic pattern of our shifting environ, assimilating it, absorbing it, internalizing it in our collective experiences, in our families at a microcosmic level, and *finally,* within our own selves, within the split halves of our individual beings," she pondered.

"*I feel like I am split into halves from within*"....

That half-formed sentence was only a glimpse of the shadow that loomed large on him. *In* him. The shadow that he had found ways of avoiding somehow. The demons that were either locked up in a strawberry jam bottle with a red and white checkered lid that he brought home on each visit or brewed slowly in a deep, rich black coffee. It was either cloyingly sweet or caustic and bitter. Shuttling between cites, going from the acrid deserts to the lush green mountains, from the backwater lagoons to the local gondola ride, the *shikara* in his lake, the demons traveled with him wherever he went.

"*I feel like I am split into halves...,*" his voice had trailed.

114

So many years later, she regretted not hugging her uncle in his moment of utter fragility. How many embraces did she regret not showering upon others? How many did she, thus, deprive herself of?

I'm split into halves.... Split...into...halves...

The split he had alluded to, was not unique to him, she realized many years later. The first trace of that split was drawn in each one of them the day they drew in their first breath, expanding their tiny, pink lungs, breaking down the barriers that separated them from all that surrounded them, their homes, their milieu, those mountains and the lakes. They were all born with those 'splintered' pieces; bits that they somehow managed to keep together, glued by the demands of love, duty, responsibility, sacrifice, anger, resentment, rebellion and what not. But then, occasionally, there would be a big bang and the pieces would be in shambles, scattered everywhere, forcing them to recognize the gaps, the broken lines, the unfilled silences, the incoherence of narratives, the dark truths, and the white lies.

These 'splinters' had found their way into the eyes of their children now, *blinding* them way before they had even been taught to see the beauty that Nature had so benevolently bestowed upon them. Pain, pathos, yearning, conflict and strife had become such constant fixtures in their lives, that they had become almost synonymous with the *very concept* of home, with the landscape of familiarity, the comfort of knowing. They had been born in a beautiful prison and never knowing what freedom meant, they desired it even more, for it seemed to signify this elusive, unattainable, evasive seductress, that couldn't be owned or possessed by them, but the addictive chasing of this *chimera* was worth every inch of their incarcerated existence! What it seemed to be doing to their collective psyche was far more dangerous, for it made masochists out of them, pain becoming such an innate part of their nature, that they couldn't possibly know what pleasure was, until *pain itself* became pleasure.

'Must I give up my love for freedom? Or must I give up all freedom for love? She laughed loudly.

115

"Stop chasing air!" her mother had admonished her, when she would spend days and nights delving upon her 'condition', ruminating and mulling over life and its unfulfilled promises, unmet expectations and undreamt dreams.

Weren't they all chasing air here? Hadn't they all been born into it?

"I feel like I have always been in a mental prison," her brother broke down, as he spoke of his mental incarceration and his spiritual immurement.

They were all caged in their own mental prisons, and having been shackled forever, they had become institutionalized too. Stockholm syndrome! That's what they all seemed to be suffering from, each one of them, including her. She was a captive of her own mind and didn't know if she truly desired liberation, until such moments when it became unbearably agonizing and she would then beg to be saved from her own self.

Hum kya chahte? Azadi!

What do we desire? Freedom!

They were shadows, each one of them, shadows of a ghost town, shadows that had been sleep walking through life, shadows that kept seeking shadows in others, chasing them, desiring them. They could love that shadow, they could dance playfully with it, they could enjoy hearty laughs with it too, but once the shadow became real, their own shadow would shrink away from it, recoiling in horror, in disappointment.

She too was wincing at the 'real, palpable, tangible' nature of love.

She too, was a shadow chasing shadows.

She too, had been somnambulating through life.

Clunk!

That metallic sound had suddenly awoken her. She had bemoaned the lack of love in her life. *All* her life. "I have to close my eyes again, for only then can I truly see!" she reprimanded herself....

Her mind was ablaze again...

Anyone that measured the vast expansive ocean of love by its indescribable, ineffable nature was only deluding himself. He was a swimmer that measured the depth of the sea by simply standing at its shore, never plunging his head in, never jumping straight inside, never as much as dipping his weak heel in that cold water. Love didn't require us to be trained swimmers, it pulled us in fiercely, no matter how strongly we resisted those raging currents and it would teach us how to, *at least,* keep our chins above the surface of water, long enough for us to survive. No, no one was an expert on love or on life. She, least of all. We all did it wrong in our own unique way

She wanted freedom. Freedom from the constricting, claustrophobic confines of love.

Hum kya chahte? Azadi!

While love had the power of making her feel like a beautiful poem sung in a heart rending, sonorous voice, the power to evoke vivid, florid imagery and the capacity to weave a dense, rich tapestry of tales, *that* was only a shadow of love, the chaff, the husk. The *real* grain, the kernel, the core, the *milk* of love, was one that had to be experienced on the plane of the mundane, in the joy of everyday, in its boring, tiring, monotonous consistency, in the travails of the quotidian, in the drudgery of daily existence. The highs of love were no more than a prelude to it, no more than the act of buying the tickets to a show--the real act of sitting through the drama, of watching it being enacted before her own eyes, with both the actors and audiences becoming one, fusing, blending, merging-- *that* was the *real* journey! And this was exhausting as hell! It drained her soul to the very hilt. In this courtroom, she embodied them all- the jury, the accused, the victim, the innocent bystanders and the Lady Justice replete with her

117

blindfolds. She, somehow had to learn to see with her eyes shut, with her ears blocked, keeping the delicate, harmonious balance within her, all the time.

I must learn to see with my eyes shut....

She seemed to be mumbling this to herself in her sleep, lest she forgot when she woke up.

With her eyes shut, she had no option left but to dive inside herself, to see inwards. And to turn that penetrating gaze onto the various halves of her own being was tormenting, it split her soul even further, with the only hope that, in the end, she could somehow understand that completion or unification was not the desired end, only a gentle recognition of the halves was. But to *sit* back and enjoy this theater required a lifetime of work. She let out an exhausted sigh. Yes, she had to keep her heart wide open to be moved by the tragedy of it, to laugh uproariously at the dark comedy of it, and in the end, a tender, discerning soul to let the various split halves go in whatever direction they wished to.

Because deep inside, they were all split into halves...

As the night inched its way towards dawn, as she still lingered on in that twilight zone between sleep and wakefulness, another random image flitted across her mind.

Another *shikara* ride. This time, the *shikara* had docked all the way up to the second storey of their house. *Jhelum* had flowed right into their 'homes', the balcony being transformed into a jetty while her old grandfather was being carried on her brother's shoulders and helped onto the boat. He crouched on the plank in the center of the boat, his rigid, old and decrepit, Parkinson's afflicted body, restricting him, neither allowing him to stand fully erect, nor sit down completely. He thus lay, frozen, suspended in a half sitting, half standing posture. As his bent silhouette receded and faded into the hazy grayness, she kept staring silently and the mist stung her eyes.

She would never forget the look in his eyes as he was slowly being rowed away...But *where?*

Those eyes, with a grey ring encircling his iris, that spoke of years passed by, of memories having accumulated in them, much like the silt that had settled in the river bed of Jhelum, causing it to overflow, memories graying-- as those old black and white photographs that had kept him awake--settling down as the grey mist of senescent eyes, those arcs of old age, *arcus senilis....*

The look in those searching eyes would haunt her forever...

Where was home now?

What was home?

Floating in the river?

unanchored, drifting away?

In whose arms? In whose lap?

On which banks?

Where was home now?

Where was home?

Several lives waiting to be lived in one,

Several scattered bits then magically reunited,

Specks of dust sprinkled and then gathered,

Tightly held in smooth pink palms.

Several lives desired in one

Castles of cards made in air

Brought down and locked in one box

A treasure trove with lost keys

A wellspring of mundane memories

Of celestial delights too

Both heavens and earth in one.

Branches sprouting in many directions, spreading out, embracing the skies

Stemming, yet, from a common Source

The Origin and the End.

Anchored by this root, boring deep into the earth

Splitting, dividing, spreading, ramifying

Creeping slowly in unseen, untried paths

Strewn with pebbles and stones and rocks

Serpentine, sinuous convolutions of the meandering mind.

Several lives lived there too

Dissipated here, there, everywhere

Now to be found nowhere.

Pale full lives lived in halves

Half a smile

Half a kiss

Tiny portions embedded in secret places

Too many doors leading up to too many places

And one long, narrow corridor to be traversed.

In light or in Dark

"I did not know what I wanted. I was afraid of life; I was driven to leave it; and in spite of that I still hoped something from it."

-Leo Tolstoy, *on his depression.*

The Lost Leaf

The pashmina of my fall

Dear Sun,

Today was a good day. As good as it gets. I'm grateful to God for the breeze that played with my hair, grateful for the weight that seemed to have been lifted off my shoulders. Yes, I felt light. I felt 'the unbearable lightness of my being.' Acutely. Yes, my shoulders did not sag under the tremendous burden that they toted. My muscles were not 'taut', they have memorized the lessons they were unknowingly 'taught.'

Yet when I return, my sadness returns. It is like a shadow that follows me around, sun or not. You follow me, Sun? I smile at the coincidence. My situation is such that I cannot fully bare my heart to you, yet I cannot somehow bear the brunt of unshared silences either. So even if it be silence,

I gingerly place it upon your palms, hoping you would understand all it hopes to convey. Read not my lines, but my heart. I keep this leaf open for you to grasp from it whatever you can. Listen. Don't fiddle with my fiddle. Don't touch those high-strung strings, for it can gash through your fingers and oh that sting!

Sun, why this 'inheritance of loss,' I ask myself? Why! I'm at a loss of words now.

Tell me, will you? How do we stop looking for the likeness of a shadow in the real form? How do we do that? What is it about unrealized dreams that they chase us even when we try not to chase them? Sun, my heart hurts. It really hurts so much at times. I try to put up a brave front, I really do. But sometimes, it catches me off guard. Sun, my soul is amid a storm yet again, one that I have been struggling with, for quite some time. It undulates around a baseline. There is an ebb and a tide, then an ebb and again a tide. And thus, I oscillate with the vacillations of my heart. From one extreme to the other. But my centre of gravity never seems to stir. I shake it. It shakes me too. But it sits still. I don't know if I'm even making any sense to you, Sun. Even if I don't, I must write. This is all I am left with now. The ruins of my words. See the macabre dance? I am so gullible, so naive. How can you fall into a trap twice over? How? The same trap. The same you. And the same fall too? I look at people around me and I marvel at their clarity of thoughts. On everything. Then I look within myself and I feel ashamed.

Of love I would never be sure, of this I always was…. I had read my Ghalib well...

'Kahun kiss se mei ki kya he, shab e gham buri bala he

Mujhe kya bura tha marna agar ek baar hota'

125

Pray how can I speak of these sad nights?
Were it but death that comes only once!

Sun, I'm putting my fire out, extinguishing it with my own hands. Come blow those verses upon my heart and snuff this candle out, will you?

Faraz echoes my pain...

'Ab tak dil e khush fahm ko tujh se hain umeedain

Ye aakhri shamme bhi bujhane ke liye aa'...

A candle of hope still flickers in the heart of a fool

Come, for no more than to blow this hope out...

Sun, what is love? I try to bring it into the realm of my present condition. Is love an ache? An inevitably earned yearning? A longing? An insufferable suffering? A sudden separation? Is love that thin, fragile line that separates two fluids not meant to be mixed? Touching gently, brushing past each other, grazing barely, imperceptibly, yet never really meeting. Two lines running parallel to each other, intersecting very briefly, only to diverge forever.

Remember the song we listened to together?

'Jaane ye kaun meri rooh ko choo kar guzra

Ik qayamat hui bedaar Khuda khair karey'

Pray who leaves having touched my soul thus?

O merciful God! What calamity has befallen me!

Why do we keep going back, extrapolating that graph over and over again in our heads? Hoping it would meet the x abcissa somewhere before the y ordinate devours it, reducing us both to zero? I think of the infinite possibilities onto my right. But I cannot lie. My gaze keeps returning to the left. That on my left. And that's when life shifts leftward for me. Life, Sun. Life... Life is not elsewhere, Sun. But here. Now. So, should be love, isn't it?

And here I find recourse in Ghalib yet again...

'Ragun mei daudte phirne ke hum nahi qayil

Jab aankh hi se na tapka to phir lahu kya he?'

What good is blood that courses through my veins

but gushes not through my eyes as tears?

What will quench my thirst? The well in the arid vastness of the desert or a mirage formed as your rays touch the hot, parched sand? The well is within reach. Within my grasp. It sleeps as I sleep and awakens as I wake up. While the mirage? It runs. Always. Never toward me, but away. It prevaricates. The lie breaks off the tie. Should I, then, not shrug off all lies? Should I drape myself in a white muslin shroud, embodying Death or should I warm my heart back to Life with my own pashmina thread? I know the roughness of the travails that would accompany the softness of the latter. I can feel it abrade my skin even as we speak. What all must I go

127

through for it! What a long, sinuous, serpentine path! How arduous the task!

I know I must find that goat, befriend it, train it, tame it too, before it will bow its head before me, ready to be sheared off.

I smile as I am reminded of Khusro yet again...

'Hum aahuwaane sehra sar e khud nihaada bar qaf

Ba ummeed aan ki roozi ba shikar khwahi aamad'...

All the gazelles of the desert shall sever their own heads,

In the hope, that one day, the hunter shall come to hunt the already hunted

For you, a gazillion times over, dear heart...This is how I fool it, Sun.

But before my hangul is hunted down, it must make itself worthy of it... So, it must be reared and fed with care...

And you know how I must feed it? It must graze not only on the grass of my existence but the roots of my grass too. And there is a lot of mud there, a lot of soil that has soiled it. What must I set out for, then? The well or the mirage? The real or the imagined? The one that is, wants to be or that which was, but never really? Well, well! Should I simply accept the fact that, as I drink from the water of this spring, the thirst of the mirage shall always remain? That it is but a hole in the whole of my existence, which gives me the possibility, the opportunity even, to fill it up with so much else? Holy God! What must we fill such an abyss with? I live in the heart

128

of a valley, I must know, mustn't I? Valley, gorge, abyss, chasm. They ought to be inscribed in my DNA.

So, the softness of my pashmina, you say? I shall be alone in that life too. As shall I be alone in my death. If I tread the oft trodden path, I will have to spin that yarn myself, the spindle will prick my finger a million times, then I must die a thousand deaths too as I dye it in my colour. And as I thrash it onto the stone on the banks of Jhelum, to wash off the excess colour, to mordant what must remain, my soul shall take a million beatings too.

I become Khusro pleading...

'Bal bal jaun mei tohe rang rajwa

Apni si rang deeni mose naina milaikey

Aisi rang do ke rang naahin chhutey

Dhobiya dhoye chaahe saari umariya'

'For you, my dyer, may I die a million times over!

You, who coloured my entire being with his glance!

A colour so deep that it never fades,

The lifelong beatings of the washer man notwithstanding!'

And then I must still stand tall

As the freezing water runs over,

My feet, my soul and my shawl

I must hang myself too on those banks,

On the nylon thread, where my shawl hangs

That drenched, crushed, crumpled drape

Each crease with a story, each line mirroring those pangs

Felt by my heart as it thirstily drank

That bitter wine made by the crushed grape

As the pigeons fly by, up in the sky

Over the pagoda of my Shah-i-Hamadan

I must iron the shawl with no hint of a sigh

Escaping my lips in memory of the yarn

That prick, the iron hot pain, that anguish, the angst

All flowed in the waters of my beloved land.

I must now, steady my gaze and my frail hand, both

As the blackness of the block inks the plainness of my shawl

I recall the walls of the shrine, those ceilings, the pillars, one and all

And imprint those paisleys, those almonds, the flowers

From the doors and windows,

Kissed, touched, and retouched at unearthly hours

Thus, that Faith finds its way from the wall, onto my shawl...

Hear now! Hush!

As the stillness of the dawn is broken by a heart rending cry

And the ripples created in Jhelum strike against those wooden planks

There, inside that sanctuary rests a lone figure

Head bowed down before Fate

Draped in a pashmina shawl

Tattered, jaded, moth eaten,

Clad thus, in the pashmina of her fall....

She sheds all patterns, all motifs now

As the chinar sheds its ripened leaves...

Stranger passes by, stops and bends over

Puts his hand tentatively over the bent figure

One push, and the body falls onto her side

The River had called her back home,

And both in Life and Death

It had been her Master, her only Guide...

The glaciers would have melted by now, you think? The rivers must have swollen. But would they have deepened too? And widened their chests to admit the sudden inflow and the gentle, imperceptile trickle? My Jhelum, my Lidder. When I dip my feet in it this time, I shall ask the rock how it fared in my absence. And I shall then share with it my own account. I must tell that story, Sun. One day, I will. I am told I cannot heal. For I cannot deal with another's pain until I have dealt with mine. But I want to tell them, that I want to heal my own pain in others. Remind me, Sun, to untie a few knots that I might have tied and forgotten about.

Daeshi aesim gundmich, wain chem mitsraavin

Remind me to untie the threads tied in faith

With my love,

As gentle as the pashmina caressing the softness of your skin

And as fluid as the river that flows in our backyard

The river that separates you from me

(Or are we on the same side of it? United thus by an invisible bridge?)

S.

She had perhaps known all the while that we lay on the same side of the bridge. However, while I was trying to hold onto the knots and noose, she derived a sadistic pleasure in watching it let go, slipping through the gaps between my fingers, the coarseness bruising my palms badly. Yet, not a single drop of blood dripped down. Perhaps this was freedom for her, perhaps this was her liberating agony.

"When there is a wound on your hand, it is for the world to see and empathize with, but when your mind is frayed, you suffer alone in ignominy."

We had both decided to suffer together. It was no conscious decision and yet, it was no coincidence. It was just meant to be. And we knowingly or *unknowingly allowed it to be. She would look over as I would attempt the act of letting go....*

Of untangling the Knots tied by her

My home-grown supplications-

both require to be watered by prayers-

but as she walks up the stoned steps

Who would pray for the flight of pigeons?

Dear Sun,

I didn't bake the cake today. Neither did I sweep the house, nor did I wipe the marble floor. I did, however, wash a bundle of clothes in the washing machine. I took that semi dried bunch in my hands and went out to hang them in the space in our backyard. This area is like a dead space that has been enclosed by an iron grill on all sides, for 'reasons of security' I believe. It reminds me so much of Kashmir. That iron grill which makes it very prison-like is the only similarity I see between here and home, so it gives me a 'feeling' of home. As I was hanging the clothes on the rope one by one, I saw a pigeon fluttering by. It had probably managed to steal its way in through the crack in the roof. It kept fluttering from one end to the other desperate to get out, yearning for the blue skies, I imagine. Having plunged in, it had somehow forgotten its way out. I felt its pain so acutely that I tried my best to catch it in my hands, so I could direct it out. I really wanted to get it out of its confinement. Pain erases pain you said. To ease your own distress, you tend to help another that appears to be in a similar state of anguish. Isn't that natural? To want to heal oneself by attempting to heal our pain reflected in others? Isn't that what you were trying to do? In wanting to embrace me, you were hugging that raw part in yourself that was not hugged. Don't we seek similarity to feel less lonely? I went inside and got some crumbs of biscuit and tried to bribe the pigeon with those. But it was too smart to fall for these tricks. It is dark now and the clothes are still hanging on the nylon rope that stretches across the iron grill. I cannot hear wings flapping wildly. The pigeon is either too tired now and has given up, resting in some corner, waiting for the sun to show it the way or it found its way home even in the dark. I really want to believe the latter. For selfish reasons, of course. Which one of the two endings (or beginnings) would you want to bet on?

You know what else was playing in my mind? I was wondering if it is possible to create light inside when everything seems dark on the outside. I was told today that courage is not the absence of fear, rather the ability to stick around despite all fears. To somehow hang in there. Just as my clothes are hanging on the thin, taut rope. People tell me, and I tell myself that all things come to a pass. This too shall pass. I know there is some truth in this. This too shall pass, as does the night give way to a new morning and the cycle goes on and on. Speaking of cycle, has the cycle of violence and bloodshed ended there?

"No soul shall carry a burden more than it can bear. Verily! With hardship comes ease." I keep reminding myself this is an opportunity for me. He wants me to do something that I didn't do right before. Hence these trials.

Dil na ummeed to nahi, na kaam hi to he

Lambi he ghum ki sham, magar sham hi to he...

The heart, dejected yet not defeated
The night, long, yet just a night...

Like Faiz, I too feel exiled from home. Exiled from my beloved Kasheer.

But I must be patient. I must show up each morning and keep going. I want to sleep now, my darling, for my eyes are heavy. Pray I sleep.

I will tell you if the pigeon ate the crumbs I left out for it.

Your friend,

S.

A 'Flight' Of Pigeon(s)

Gently, gently into the arms of the Dark Night,

No fragrance fills those blackest recesses,

No crushed rose petals embrace her fragile body,

smeared red or dabbed white,

Tender lullabies wafting in the air,

sweet little nothings whispered in her ear,

tiny rusty tin soldiers tinkling away,

a singular tone amiss, a phantom limb severed

No dreams console her, no ice flakes rest on her droopy lids no dewdrops on petals, no pillows soaked

On endless treks through the snowy peaks, treads she

Uphill, uphill, uphill.

Pine cones cup her tender heart--a savage beast, this cunning fox

Lone tendrils curling up her blue feet, frostbitten and cold

a solitary needle nestled in her bosom

Heart clutched, heart seized, diseased, deceased

One clenched fist, one iron grip

One soft hand opening her palm....

finger by finger by finger,

And Lo! The pigeon flies!

She was so full of paradoxes. Contrasting, conflicting contradictions defined her, in fact, extruded her, ousting her away from the ambit of any '*definite, defined*' definition. She could either be *nothing* or *everything,* running on an *'all-or-none'* law, the cursed outlaw! Damn those nerves! How they tricked her! Tragic! Not that it was the only tragedy that had befallen her. Or them. In a split second, you could see the whole universe collapse before your disbelieving eyes, all existence turning to naught, hers and that of those that she engulfed in the arms of the fire that seemed to emanate from within her, all hell breaking loose. *A pandemonium*, make no mistake! And in the *same second* perhaps, you could witness a rebirth, a slow, painful delivery back from the Jaws of Death, a perilous oscillation between this world and that, with a thin, fragile line separating one from the other. This line blurred sometimes, frightening her beyond measure, becoming almost imperceptible and nonexistent on days-days, dark and painful, days, turning into months. *Life. Death. Rebirth.* And the cycle repeated itself. This cycle needed to be broken for the sake of sanity! For the sake of *reason,* perhaps? What *needed* to be done, she supposed, was *this:* With the center remaining constant, she needed to expand her circle infinitely, so that the boundary that separated her from the outside world thinned, until it ceased to exist, so she could achieve oneness with herself, an ultimate act of self-embrace, of life embracing life, life welcoming life.

Her head was full of vague, abstract ideas, so full, that it hurt unbearably at times. And what all resided in that little head of hers, who could tell? Not her, for sure! Such formless, shapeless thoughts as could be poured into any vessel of any shape. She could fill pitchers and pitchers of wet, moist clay with nothing. Yet the beauty of it could be unearthed in the simple fact, that this seeming *nothing* could be seen in *any* form one wished. *That* power lay in the seeking eyes. One could see a reflection of what one desired to see. No! Not desire! Perhaps what one *needed* to see. This mirror was life itself, shrunk and polished until it shined back at her. And like life, this mirror decided what her eyes were fit to see and *when* and what needed to be carefully hidden from her inexperienced, uninitiated eyes. This mirror was her heart too. Autonomous, unruly, rebellious and refusing being reined in, or being tamed- stubborn and obstinate, yet, hopelessly fragile and brittle.

139

The world was turning blind and here she was writing about seeing impossible visions! "Fool!" she rapped at her own knuckles in anger.

Of all the possible images that her mirror was reflecting, there had been a few recurrent ones that she needed to be erased. *For good*. For they threatened to *blind* her with their immense blackness.

She took a long, deep breath in, exhaling very softly and using the tip of her index finger, began rewriting on the misty mirror.Her own story retold in her own words; Seeds scattered in the wind to be carried away wherever the soil was fertile, and she could *then*, write on the silvery bark of the birch tree dotting her *Meadow Of Gold*, her *Sonamarg,* using the lucid, pristine waters *of Nallah Sindh,* as her ink, as *she had, such a long time ago…*

But for *that* she had to wait, for those waters were carmine still…

Another day was nearing its end. Another evening was slowly taking over. Another night of the same old life.

And, in all this, as she settled down, in a familiar corner carefully marked by her, pen in hand, thinking about what to write, she found herself suddenly paralyzed by fear, gripped and seized by an indomitable realization. There had been days when stories would simply ooze out of her pores, days when songs could be written, when words would wind around whorls of laughter, chiming in the breeze of free flowing tales, words sagging under the burden of pain, words beaming with love, sprinkled with bitterness, dabbed with misery even, soaked in the monsoon rains, blooming in spring, like fresh almond blossoms swaying in the wind, words ground and mixed with the smell of flowers, words seasoned with spices, betrayed by a friend, abandoned by a lost lover, dying a thousand deaths, words buried, words reborn. But then! One day. One day the rivers would simply dry up. And then, there would be no new stories to tell. She quivered at the mere thought!

After all, how long could this static water withstand the intensity of the scorching, blazing sun? Tiny tributaries having branched out, extracting portions from this source, taking away from it, draining it out, until it would shrink slowly, becoming diminutive, and then the dry, ugly underbelly of *Jhelum* would be exposed.

What, then, would she do! She gasped and wrung her hands in despair.

Wherefrom could one find the means to replenish those reservoirs? Which branch of a miracle tree could be bent slightly, easily and new juicy stories would be plucked from them like ripened cherries? Which mysterious well could be chanced upon by a thirsty woman to quench her thirst? She would patiently, perseveringly, pull out bucketsful of this sparkling water, laboring over the ragged rope rolled around the pulley, creaking noisily. This hard toil would have been no deterrent to her, whatsoever. Once she had had her fill, she would wait for the well to fill up again, slowly-at its own pace, on its own will. For the stories chose their writer and not the other way around, she strongly believed.

Words had an inherent tendency to *home* to their natural habitats. *They would home to their home, eventually.* They could not be tamed or reined in, or spoken *for*, or even spoken *out!* She laughed. They simply could not be made to walk in a straight line, like a bunch of disciplined, obedient school kids, or be made to bend at the desired curves with the flick of our presumptuous pens. No way! They made their own path, they chose their own roads and the destination too, and at best, she could simply follow their cue and keep holding onto her end of the thread as they pulled her in sudden jerks or simply made her wait upon them in the freezing cold, barefoot, hours on end. *They* were the ones that were capricious and whimsical, not her, and she had no choice but to accept this. To surrender her pen to it, and bow her head down, silently. Without a *word* uttered, she smiled and so she submitted without a 'protest,' for what if there would be no stories left to tell?

"No! No! It can't be!" she shuddered, she had to let her words, if not her, home to their home...

What do I write about tonight?

when there is nothing left inside

when all the stories have flowed out as rivers of tears…

What do I write about tonight?

when the head and heart are empty

and the soul is starved

Tiny saplings deprived of water and light…

What do I write about tonight?

when the insides are knotted tight

when the heart is walled off from the rest

and the soul is repeatedly put to test

What do I write about tonight?

Songs of grief and mourning?

Of living dead thrown in graves?

graves dug out surreptitiously

in the dead of the night…

What do I write about tonight?

Hopes laid to rest?

Wings clipped off before they were spread?

Lines erased before they were read?

What do I write about tonight?

Wails stifled, silenced, suppressed?

Desperate, pleading, agonizing cries muffled

As her mouth rests on his tear stained shoulders

his hand patting her disheveled hair

rocking her body to and fro like a child's…

What do I write about tonight?

Sunken, hopeful, praying eyes searching for lost smiles?

eager ears straining to hear her laughter?

Or the fiery orange moon spotted by hollowed out eyes?

so close they could almost stretch their arms and grasp it

So close, yet so removed…

This long, dark night seems interminably long

And with the break of dawn, all their dreams were broken

shattered bits piercing their hands

Together, they pick up those sharp bits again,

pieces of their own lives in shambles

shards of glasses buried deep in both hearts

They try to salvage fragments,

those miniscule halves of halves

hoping to make this hole whole again

They toil tirelessly with all their might…

What else can I write about tonight?

for there is nothing left inside…

and nothing left to write….

The only time that she was truly awake, anchored firmly *in the moment*, was when the pointed tip of her pen touched the eagerly awaiting blankness of white paper sprawling before her. At least someone else was as blank and clueless as her! What a relief that provided! She could never predict what she would write about, never really could direct the course of any sentence, any line that stemmed forth, simply of its own accord. These were sand dunes that formed and shifted with the sudden changes in the desert winds, winds that appeared out of nowhere and changed the entire topography of the arid deserts, making familiar landscapes unrecognizable in a fraction of a second, intimate friends suddenly becoming complete strangers. The same uncertain winds kept blowing back home as she shuddered in cold with each gust reaching her here. Was it possible to turn a 'blind' eye to what was happening *around* her, *within* her? The word blind suddenly made her rub her eyes fiercely, as if to remind herself she was still lucky she could see.

But could she *truly see*? Could all those that had eyes truly *see*?

"What do eyes have to do vision?" she sighed. If *only* they could *see*!

All she knew, however, was *this*-it was of *utmost* importance that she writes. It was a lifesaving drug administered to the critically ill, a frantic attempt to bring the dead back to life, a resuscitation of souls (hers had long been decaying now).

"How long can I hold on?" She wondered, as she kept embalming the last remains of her words, wrapping those shriveled up, mummified creatures in the white bandages of her journal.

Would they be buried in an unmarked grave or would they be enshrined in a tomb where mothers would come to wail, kissing those walls as if kissing their children's foreheads, letting out their pain?

"I really hope that this letter never gets to you, because if it does that means I am dead."

> **- Gunner Lee Thornton**, *who was killed aged 22 in Iraq in 2006, wrote to his fiancé Helen*

One last time and then no more

this was the promise she made to herself

One last time does the mother hug her child

and sings sweet lullabies

to that body turned cold

One last time her heart bleeds

beating fiercely, madly, wildly

pressed against that heart gone silent

breathing life from her lips to his

in a desperate bid to revive her own soul

But the dead could never be brought back to life

and *that* was the truth, this mother was to learn

Her old, decrepit, deformed hands

give her baby one last bath

She scolds no more and frowns not

upon seeing his limp body

smeared with blood, mud and grime

One last act of washing all sins

of blotting all that darkness away

One last time and then no more

She reiterates her promise to herself

One last kiss planted on his velvety forehead

One last smile as she sees his angry lines have vanished

One last loving glance cast upon that mouth

that still smiles a sad smile

now cemented and captured forever

One last brush of her lips against his

as she tries to suck that coldness away

One last embrace to absorb all that pain

before she lays his head to rest…

One sudden contraction felt in her heart

as the flower of her womb was to become a seed again

buried deep under the damp ground…

One last story whispered in his ears

to keep all those demons at bay

One last time does Death Embrace Death

One last time and then no more…

Her mind, brimming till the very edge, needed a release. It was so full, so drained too, so *fully drained* now. And it is here that she was pouring all that blinding angst out. In one fierce torrent. And the emptiness of paper was the only vessel that seemed to have a limitless capacity to absorb all that she was purging out of herself. It was cathartic, yes, for this was one receptacle that kept on accepting and accommodating whatever flew into it -both roaring cascades, frothy and white, or tiny globules dribbling by, painfully slowly, barely reaching the corners of her parched open mouth. No questions were asked of her, no explanations were demanded and no 'proof of her identity' was required here. The journal had become one constant companion that she carried with her everywhere she went. These were ears that could hear and had the depth to understand what even she did not. And they had eyes that could see, *truly see* into her heart.

It had witnessed so much before as well, hadn't it? It had borne the brunt of volcanic eruptions on days, blotted and sucked away all the pain too. And now it was embracing mundane, banal nothings. It was a bearer of all her highs and lows-from the wondrous, exalted, sublime and transcendent to the ordinary, prosaic, ridiculous and base. It could open its heart to welcome both, embracing her contrasts in one tight clasp. It had the infinite capacity to heal, she had been told. She was following her prescription ritually, without fail. It was no magic wand, however. Or was it? What it essentially seemed to be doing was this--it listened to her grave silences, it took note of those *silent graves* too. It took account of the slightest of changes in her countenance, it recorded and saved all that she had to say. To herself, to the world later, perhaps? When the world would be ready to hear her. For the while, it traced the trajectory of her life for her, a life lived in exile... banished from home, exiled from self...

And *now,* she wrote for no one else, but *herself....* And this was *her* soliloquy...

152

When the storm is over, we shall then look deep and hard

into what remains and what all was lost

We shall walk the tightrope that stretched for days and nights

across my temples unyielding, taut, tight

We shall witness, then, the remains of the carnage

that dead grey ash shall kiss my feet

as I shall trace my terrain gutted down in the fire

Barefoot shall I walk in those narrow, crooked lanes

as my gaze shall bear witness

to that destruction, that desolation

And if the eyes still retain

their vision, that insight

I shall remember, forever, the misery, that plight

when Darkness was defeated in one last fight

Dear Sun,

Something very profound happened today. I am describing it to you as I heard it from my friend. She moved me to tears. I know you shed tears back in Kashmir, for entirely different reasons.

'The prayer room.' That's what it was called. One had to exit the main building of the hospital, wade through a sea of ailing, sick men and women to reach the main entrance. The 'prayer room' was at the basement. A ramp led you to it. A ramp, probably, aimed to make the passage easily accessible for the patients on wheelchairs or else on trolleys, so their path to God would be unencumbered. After all, when everything else failed, all science and medicine, one needed God. He was the ultimate Healer.

I dragged her feet along that ramp, with metallic beams embedded at regular intervals along it, as if placed knowingly to slow down the pace of desperate men and women seeking divine intervention. So, they didn't fall as they lunged forward and sprinted, in a last-ditch attempt, to pray for their loved ones.

The ramp that connected science and God. The downhill path that bridged the divide between the seen and the Unseen, a link between reason and faith, the threshold between this world and a gateway to the other.

I dragged my feet along that ramp....

I was glad for the sun, for having been cloistered in a tiny room devoid of any window was beginning to make me feel claustrophobic. It was a relief to breathe some un-conditioned fresh air and feel the winter sun on the back of one's neck. I took slow, deliberate steps along the ramp, turned at the only bend and sauntered along. To my right was a room full of steel almirahs stacked with old files to the very top. This was the medical records section where each patient's file found its resting place. Files replete with all the necessary details-- patients' particulars, their diagnoses, course of illnesses and treatments received along with the

154

outcomes. Many files carried a death certificate as well, for among those who entered, many would not make it back.

The room adjacent to this was where I was heading--the 'prayer room.' I took my shoes off at the threshold, carefully kept them aside and entered barefoot. On the left were symbols of various names of the Divine. Straight ahead on a steel almirah full of various religious texts were many folded prayer mats. I took one. The roughest of the lot. A jute mat with three borders, one inside the other, white, black and light brown from the outermost to the innermost respectively.

As I began muttering under my breath in slow, deliberate tones, I closed my eyes and let myself be immersed in it completely, my hands becoming heavy and limp. I had been restless. I closed my eyes because what I feared the most then was darkness--the uncertainty of not knowing, fear of the unseen. And that darkness was devouring my present. This fear was making me die every single second. As tears rolled down my cheeks, my heart seemed to be saying.... "I feel tired. I feel broken. Lead me ashore. Deliver me out of my pain, for only You can. Help me help myself."

The sound of glass bangles clinking and anklets chiming, and tinkling signaled that I was not alone anymore. Two women flanked me, one on either side. And as that musical sound filled the room, I knew I had to let go...I had to let go off myself and drift with the music that played around me.

Rumi says "Wash yourself of yourself"...

I had to break my old glass bangles and extend my hands forward for a set of new ones. I had to cup my hands further upwards, so He could fill it with His Goodness. I had to keep both my ears and heart open, for His tinkle could be heard in places unheard of....

As it did now, in their bangles and their anklets...

Jingle... Jingle... Jingle...

This story made my eyes well up with tears. I tell myself I miss home. I miss my Kashmir. I will come back soon.... And we can sit on the rocks in Lidder and hear the jingle of the river gushing by...

Yours

S.

Lying down on the pyre,

waiting for the last twigs to crumble to ash

The fire that consumes the mind

those agonizing flames that leap from within

Bodies were charred in that fire

black soot was smeared across the skies

as hands were thrown into those flames

to retrieve whatever could be saved...

Hands folded, she lay within that grave

as voices struck against her skin turned cold

That ugly carcass was laid bare again and again

and fingers were poked into her wound

fountains of pain oozed out again

All pain would dry up one day for good

and the dead shall then, be allowed to rest...

"Write of Hope tonight," he pleaded

"Of Hope?" her voice quivered

Hope that I shall carry in my heart

the fragrance of saffron fields, wherever life takes us?

those purple flowers in full bloom

resplendent in the silver streaks of that night

That night of full moonlight

That night she had dreamt of in dreams

That night which cast a shadow on

All her silent nights...

Yet, how could it be?

How could it be?

That no crocuses did her eyes see?

those soft hues of lilac

evaded her every season

for short lived was that heavenly blossom

It came and went before she knew

what reached her end were only threads

Those dried, rust and crimson threads

that alluded in muted, whispered tones

to the glory of what had really shone

Unseen, unobserved that spectacle had died

And what remained were threads plucked up and dried...

She lifts a handful in her hands

and ties them at the corner of her shawl

To carry the memory of blossoms that went by

Unseen by her blinded eye...

"Try, try once again", he said

"Write of Hope, dear love," he begged

"Hope, you say?" her eyes seemed to ask

Hope that the chill of this snow

shall never dim that faint, dying glow

that still burns beneath the coal

She lifts those embers, almost extinct now

and carries them in her palms

to warm her nights

so, her eyes could dream

dreams of sparkling streams

dotted with crocuses on either side...

"Sing a song of harvest," he beseeched

Of Love and laughter

Of Hope and Dreams

"Hope? Hope, you say?"

Hope that my burdened bent back shall not impede

that fiery speed

with which you chase

the dream of your dreams?

Hope that even as my heart is lost

in these deserts, endless and vast

we shall still, one day, find our way

find our way back home

all the way from the start

with the only light left

The Light of the Heart...

For with blinded eyes, we cannot see

And even with eyes, they never let us be....

He kept staring endlessly at his hands, bending those long, slender fingers this way and that, deepening the creases in the hollow of his palms, a habit she had begun to get nervous about, he would be lost in perusal for hours. She had begun believing that he could read his palm like the book lying open next to him, just as easily, just as adeptly. The lines that made no sense to her, seemed to speak to him in some secret, esoteric language. He strained his bespectacled eyes, dulled by long, tormenting nights of insomnia, as he pored over the lines of his hands. He seemed to be examining them so meticulously, so methodically as if he were examining one of his patients; a terminally sick one at that, wounded, blinded, in agony, one that required his utmost, pressing love and attention. After all, he was such a natural at being attentive to others' maladies. It was these same hands which he had placed on many mothers' shoulders, steadying them as he broke the news of their children's imminent deaths. Hands that could reflexively write down long lists of medicines to be administered to the sick and the wasted; hands, that had pierced people's spinal canals, that had passed needles and trocars through people's chests to drain off any fluid that might have collected in those cavities. "These are the same hands," she thought to herself. "Where could he possibly empty the rivers that had flooded his own heart? Rivers that had burst open all floodgates, gushed forth at raging speed and inundated everything. Whose hands would give him that gentle nick to let out the mingled pain?" She wondered.

No, he could not possibly decipher the cryptic meaning of those lines. If he could, he would have anticipated fate, both his and hers. And no man, with such prior knowledge, would deliberately put himself through all that pain. He valued life too much to be masochistic. No, it just couldn't be! He was no fortune-teller, no palmist. Even he had no inkling of what was happening both without and within. He too, like all of them, was *blind*.

But what if, he knew? What if he could tell?

Well, in any case, the coward that she was, she lacked the courage to ask him what might be written in her palms. What stories might spring forth, who could tell? But then again, who needed to even search her hands to know of the secrets that lay in her heart? Her face was hardly inscrutable, all tales were writ large over it, in her sad countenance, in her sleep deprived eyes, to be read by all, friends and foes alike, those *with* or *without* eyes. Even a stranger could just glance through her 'book' laid open.

As for her hands? That constant, agonizing, feverish wringing seemed to have erased all her lines.

She cast a glance at her palms and was startled by its expansive emptiness. "How life had simply slipped through these fingers," she thought, as tears rolled down her pale cheeks....

Into the Dark Night…

Night, take her into your comforting arms

and suck all the anguish away

her childlike body will be rocked to sleep

all the shadows of the day shall shrink away

Night, soothe those nerves gone awry

breathe life into her cold, marbled lips

dry withered skin that peels off from her lips

will be lost in the darkness of her unconscious nights

all history past, all present tales lost too

But rolled tightly as parchments of stories

with the blackness of the night having inked upon them

those tales...those unheard tales, letter by letter

could then, be told and retold

before the day kisses them goodbye again...

Night shall take her back in its arms

after yet another blinding day...

run its slender, dark fingers through her black hair

and soon all darkness shall be washed away...

Her limp, weightless body shall be lifted in those arms

and carried into the arms of yet another dawn...

Slowly.... Gently....Delicately

There were moments in her life when voice became noise, a constant clamor in her head, an unbearable din, that terrible *knock-knock* felt against the hollow cranium. *Rap... Rap... Rap...* Her mind had an eerie capacity to weave a dense web of thoughts only to find itself caught within it, entangled hopelessly in a messy net of her own creation, a master losing freedom at the hands of its own slave, and the slave enslaving her was so hard to describe...

Random... Abstract...Shapeless...

Those hot vapors rose from some place unknown and filled her nostrils with its fumes, carrying the mystique of an unattainable, highly desirable woman -tempting, seductive and alluring. There were those that knew her by those attributes. *Just that* and no more. For them, she was the vile witch that could charm the most unyielding of hearts with a slight bend in her crooked little finger. Staring blankly straight back at you with eyes that were ghostly and bewitching, terribly dead and terribly alive all at once, she could make men go mad with frenzy. They drank the sweet nectar of those lips, dreamt her dreams, lying naked next to her body, sucked out all her hopes, drank her blood, had their fill and moved on.

They skimmed her surface and delved not an inch deeper. They retained all reason and sanity quite reasonably well, once freed from the clutches of that harlot. They sang long paeans to her beauty and grace while in bondage, filled pages and pages with their panegyrical tribute to her wisdom, eulogizing her poise, elevating her status to the Sacred, the Divine. All that could bode very well with her, except that the eyes that saw all this and no more, lacked *one* vital thing, the magic ingredient, a secret hidden from most eyes. Those eyes lacked kindness, compassion and empathy. They were veiled to the point of being blind. And through those thousand and one veils, they could appreciate nothing more than her exterior--the form, the body, the shape and the imperfections.

Those 'eyes' would itch with the grain of arrogance that had sought to camouflage 'love for self' with 'selfless love.' Her eyes too, were to become red and watery, for that grain had settled inside them as well and so they would suddenly well up with tears and she was made to rub her eyes repeatedly, until that grain would be found in her eyes no more. She had to learn to soften those sharp edges with love and kindness, to smoothen the thorny, prickly, pointed surface with the lacquer that could only flow from within her heart. And layers upon layers of that shiny enamel would then give birth to the most beautiful of pearls.

This is what he was unknowingly teaching her, as he wiped the tears that singed her cheeks, each time they rolled down. Her coarse grain was to become a pearl, concealed from all disbelieving, groping, _blind_ eyes...And this painfully arduous and recondite process was to repeat itself over and over again, until would be formed in the oyster of her tender heart, that strong, iridescent, resilient jewel...The humble white pearl... And so, she strung all imperfections within herself, one tiny pearl after another, and tied the knot at the end, _firmly_. The frayed ends of her mind too, were to become beauty divine... And the blaring noise, that clamorous cacophony was to become voice, nay, music again!

She smiled through her tears as she kept rubbing her eyes like a child. Soon she was laughing as she placed her head softly on his chest, her ear next to his heart, listening to the rhythm of that music in rapt attention.

"The irritant grain was soon to become a bright, opalescent pearl," she repeated to herself, as she slowly drifted to sleep...

Chapter 4

The Smell That Lingered On

That peculiar smell still lingered on in her nostrils, long after she had left the place. She had been shoved out of that perilous, dangerous den. *Rescued*, in fact. And she had run for the life of her, as fast as her mind could allow, for her acute sense of olfaction had thrown her into a tizzy. She had been caught unawares, a bolt out of the blue had hit her right across her heart. Her once proud little nose (by no measure little!) had finally trapped her. Her nose was to become her undoing in the end. She had panicked beyond control and her facial muscles had involuntarily contracted, dancing and contorting wildly, drawing lines where none existed and deepening those that had always been there. She thought she would faint. How many times during the day did she feel thus! As those pearls of sweat were beading on her wrinkled forehead and downturned lips, he had caught her in the act. Sensing her fear, seeing that crazed look in her eyes, he had grabbed her arm and pulled her out, swiftly. Out of the way of danger, he thought.

But the smell had lingered on...

That peculiar, unique smell of new paper, crisp and white, with the black ink having touched it, forming those magical letters that had once leapt out of the pages and jumped at her, frightening her at first, until she had formed a deep, enduring bond with them, drinking from their cup and letting herself dissolve in that ocean, drop by drop, bit by bit, weaving a dense weave of tales--those crisscrossed stitches, that rich, interwoven, delicate and lacy network. This mysterious meshwork had cast its net upon her heart, entrapping and enmeshing it forever. She thus lay struggling with herself, trying to free her heart from the web that had ensnared it, eons ago, enslaving and imprisoning her, to this day.

And now as she looked back, it seemed to her like another life, another time, another her too. How quickly those years had passed her by, as if time had crystallized so abruptly that she found herself unable to keep up with its lightning speed and so she froze, trapped underneath the massive iceberg of forgotten years, years that had simply brushed past her. Years of her *own* life, a life lived in absence, in longing, in the arms of old memories. She had been hopelessly locked in those narrow, constricted interstices, with no hope of that ice melting, to free her from her chillingly cold confinement. She felt as if she was trying really hard to see her own image in a mirror that had been blanketed by a thick curtain of dust settling on it, dust gathered due to years of cruel abandonment, the dust of heartless indifference, of a loveless life, of her youth being stolen away, while she was sleeping in her bed, dreaming of a new morning, a different life. And as she woke up from her slumber, she found herself having aged beyond recognition. She moved her fingers to trace the wrinkles that had been engraved on her softened, pliant face, trying to link the breaks in her disjointed life, attempting to rewrite the story she had missed out on, the story of her own life.

But the only recognizable 'belonging' of the past, the only familiar 'face', in a completely changed, strange new world, was that of this old friend, the books she had pored over back home, as the world surrounding her had been on the boil. And she simply closed her eyes, to let her nose take on the job at hand. She knew what she had to do. She had to recount her story using her olfactory prowess.

With no sight, that was *all* that had stayed with her, *all* that still remained…

The faint smell that still lingered in her nostrils…

That unique aroma had caged her heart in a tight claustrophobic armor ever since she had first stumbled upon it. "Was it the peculiar smell of those letters that stamped my heart forever?" she wondered. Or was it the quaint uniqueness of strangers' hands flipping through those pages admixing with the stories hidden inside, the sweat of eager fingers leafing through them, leaving distinct individual odors behind, losing all individuality, becoming suddenly indistinct, blending, fusing and mingling with the smell of her words. The resultant fragrance was so striking, so characteristic, so intimate that it could have been no mere accident. No, she hadn't simply *chanced* upon it. It was no serendipitous meeting of long lost lovers destined to be together. It carried the whiff of a master perfumer, the skill of a seasoned sorcerer, the charms of an enchanter and the sharpness of a magician. It was an artist's creation, a labor of love. The magic of mixing the right ingredients in the right proportions could be attained only after years and years of practice. Or perhaps not even then. "It was an alchemy unto itself," she yawned.

"But who was this sculptor of carefully chiseled words?"

Her eyes began closing and slowly, sleep overtook her.

And there she lay in the arms of her own memories again, undressing her own thoughts, exposing her soul in all its nakedness, shedding one layer of consciousness after another, while her subconscious took her up those flight of stairs, one step at a time--the staircase leading to heaven.

She still had blindfolds on her eyes, she was blind as a bat, but she let herself be guided forth by the light of her heart (*weinji gaash*) and by the sharp acuity of her nose. And *there*, she could still smell it all, from the floral fragrance of her romance--light, weightless and slightly sweet, the nectar collected from roses, violets, lilies and jasmines; to the woody heaviness of her tragedy--the musky smell of sandalwood; the fresh scent of her comedy--acidic, citric, acerbic--oranges and lemons squeezed in her head, fruity and playful, and finally, the oriental fragrance of far-away exotic lands-- spicy, warm and sensual, the smell of peppers, cloves and cinnamons rubbed on her bare skin.

And then, she woke up with a start.

Those smells had still lingered on, yet they smelled different... definitely different... She could smell that change in the air, these were the winds of change he had promised her of, before he had left her that fateful morning without a word.

She was to be that wind of change, she smiled as she wiped the dusty mirror with her hands.

He had left so suddenly, deserting her and forcing her to fend for herself, to nurse her wounds herself, *alone*. And now that he had returned, she felt bitter, angry and sad. No, she couldn't let her heart go through the torment that it had yet not completely resurfaced from. She simply refused being evicted out of another home--a nest that she had tried to make, gathering each tiny straw, each little twig--a home away from home. She clung onto dear life, clutching her heart, in a fencing, pugilistic posture, ready to rip him apart. She kept waiting for him to break his silence first.

"I must not even give him the pleasure," she thought to herself.

No, she wouldn't complain, sound pathetic or grovel before him.

The air between them was so heavy, so solid that she felt she could cut it with a knife into two. But she held her heart and her ground, both.

He kept looking at her, uttering not a word.

And all it took was one moment.

One miniscule fraction stolen from the watchful, sentinel eyes of life, one infinitesimally small second to break all barriers that had barricaded their hearts, that had shielded one from the penetrating, loving gaze of the other, creating a staggeringly tall fortress around them, isolating, insulating, sequestering and segregating a diseased, ailing heart; a heart that had been quarantined for God-knows-how-long. Transforming *that*, which was meant to be a porous vessel of clay-- receiving a gentle trickle of love, allowing it to seep into its depths and then distilling it out in a greater, purer form--into an iron cauldron, rigid, fixed and impervious to everything, receiving nothing and giving out nothing. The thread that stretched between them, that lifeline running across ends which was meant to infuse, enrich and expand the other, had snapped somewhere along the way.

In such tainted, *tinted* times, even *they* had become blind, blind to each other, blind to kindness and blind to love.

172

Yet all it had taken to rejoin those split, frayed ends was one embrace. One interminably long embrace, one millisecond captured in stillness, one fleeting, evanescent moment, one light touch that transcended bodies. They clutched onto each other for what seemed to be a second, hoping against hopes, for all time to freeze, for it to stretch to an eternity, as if the simple act of holding each other, with abandon, a total surrender of souls, that unrestrained, uninhibited touch could transmit more than just warmth from one heart to the other.

As they held each other, nothing was said, yet *all* was understood. That pristine, unblemished silence was pregnant with meaning, meanings that defied the limitations put by speech, meanings that rebelled against the captivity of words, meanings that floated freely, expanded at will, grew of their own accord... free spirits dodging bondage, refusing enslavement...The clarity that came with such voicelessness was so sacred, so profound that it could not be tarnished by the flaws imposed by the imperfect speech of imperfect mortals.

To say nothing then, was to say it all....

Don't break this river of silence

Don't break it up into tiny little fragments

Don't break it by words thrown carelessly around

or even those carefully thought out

Don't break this linear thread

Don't break it at all

Don't break this silent poetry

Don't stack up words one atop the other

for this delicate deck of cards might simply fall

Don't break this silence today

Don't break it at all

Hide those eager notes of music carefully under the bed

Let them learn the dance of silence

Don't fling them straight ahead

They are nascent, unformed yet

Don't pluck those inchoate buds too early

Don't force these flowers open

Let them soak in the rains of silence

Don't put your hands around them,

Don't encase them

Don't break this river of silence

Don't break it just yet...

She was going about her chores perfunctorily. It seemed as if someone had pushed the 'on' button and there she was, whirring away noisily. "Some machine!" she thought. "Not even a well-oiled one!" she sighed. Oh! If only she could function smoothly, waltzing in and out of these transitions effortlessly, like an elegant, instinctive dancer, replete with a sensuous, shapely, arched back, lovely curves, perfect pirouettes, carefree sways, pointed toes, magnificent like those staggeringly tall poplars back home in Kashmir that danced gracefully in the breeze. What a breathtaking sight that would make! She caught the corner of her downturned mouth curl up only slightly. Yes, see she hadn't forgotten it after all! She could still initiate a smile. And there, it vanished before she could fully bask in the glory of that victory

"These muscles were supposed to be voluntary, weren't they?"

She bared her teeth and felt the mask stretch painfully across her face. No, this wasn't good enough, it had to come from within.

She was packing a suitcase. She wanted to wind up everything, pull off the curtains in one sudden thrust and shove all her belongings shut. All these layers, this elaborate tapestry was so unnecessary. These were appendages she didn't need. They served no purpose. She had to quickly shut the suitcase tight before those ghosts would rise up again from the dead. She hastened to lock it and now all she had to do was wait. Wait to go. But *where*? There was nowhere to go, nowhere to run or hide. She had to teach herself to be. Just *be.* With or without suitcases. With or without ghosts.

"Be here. In the moment. Present. Alive. Mindful of each breath you take," she advised herself.

But right now, she just wanted to run, run as fast as her feet could take her. She wanted to sprint across those luscious meadows of dreams, she wanted to immerse herself fully in the imagery her mind evoked. It had such tremendous power, such unchallenged authority on her heart, as only one that knew her insides could know. Here, she could see it all, feel it, taste it, drink it. She could feel the warmth of the summer sun on her back as she imagined it. She could conjure up the fragrance of daffodils and lilies and smell the smell wafting slowly, finding its way to her nostrils. She could shiver in the icy coldness too, as she sat in the scorching sun. *Could anyone see her hair stand on end as her feet felt cold? Could they feel the chill as it ran down her spine? Could they see those toes change color as they became cyanosed?*

No, she wasn't blue at all! It was her toes. Not *her*. Not at all!

She shook her head sideways.

She poured all her angst in wiping the floor. She wanted it clean, spotless, unmarred and sparkling. So, dazzling that she could see her image reflected at her, so she could see all that she saw in her mind's eye being translated onto the floor. The floor was her reticent retina. In that green and white marble, those smooth-edged rhomboids inter-digitating with each other, she hoped for her dark shadow to simply glide away. If she scrubbed and polished it well, she would surely see in it all that she hoped to see. She would become that floor, those opaque green and white pieces and she could then, slowly become transparent. Softened, yet multifaceted--scintillating, coruscating diamond, the jewel that lay buried within her heart. She just had to keep rubbing at the colored, tinted surface. If only she kept scrubbing it well! She had to remove all that excess glaze that it had acquired, she had to hone it till she reached the very core, till all that flesh would be removed and she could, then, reach the bone. No, reach the marrow in fact. Oh, she was being too ambitious! Too ambitious too soon!

"Rub! Rub! Rub, all you can silently," she reminded herself.

"Was there a method to it? Could someone please delineate the steps again?"

She would follow it to a T, if only someone read out those secret verses from the book.

Her mind wandered again. In the repetitive movements of her arms, it found its gaps, it made its way, slowly but surely, just as a stream found its path through the pebbles, *around* them, hooking *over* them. She could trace the history of each stain on the floor, she could extrapolate it right till her heart. She knew exactly where Madhu's red toe ring had struck against the cold marble. Madhu wore the ruby of her heart in her toes. She had abhorred it at first, hadn't she? And now, she could hear the tinkle in her ears long after Madhu had left. She wanted to hold Madhu by her arm when she came and go around in circles of joy. No, she mustn't do that! Madhu would think her to be crazy, crazier than she already does.

As she picked up the strands of her hair from the floor, she stretched them out to see if she could smoothen the bends. They would get taut and then, as she slowly released her grip, they fell back onto the floor—curled and wavy, black threads against the milky whiteness of the floor. These were the coiled threads of conversations that never took place, conversations that would curl up upon themselves. They had to be given the vast open skies of silence, they would soar high in that sapphire firmament. Some things had to be left as they were, after all. They were prettier that way. She pulled all those stray strands in one swift movement and threw them in the yellow dustbin.

Her mother had left. But the tree that she had eagerly pointed out to her daughter before she left, still bore the orange flowers.

"Those black bunch of grape like seeds burst open into an orange blossom," she had told her.

They were tiny bells hanging on their balcony, tinker bells that would carry the tinkle of her mother's voice, her soothing music. If only she could grab a pen and write down that symphony, or maybe gulp its nectar down in one go and then summon it whenever she needed the intimacy of that voice and the comfort it afforded her on silent days.

Did life work that way? Could she be *here, there, everywhere*? Could she be a part of laughter shared in her absence? Could secret glances cast in complicity reach her here? Perhaps, they could. She believed in the oneness of all sounds, didn't she?

She was humming, humming in her head as she washed the cups.

"If only I were poetry in motion or perhaps a soulful song? If only I could play like a beautiful, lyrical and well-orchestrated musical piece!"

But here she was- coughing, breaking and sputtering so often, slouching, with not even the slightest hint of grace.

"Why did my shoulders droop so?" she exhaled.

Yes, she was nursing and clutching her wounded heart, trying her best to protect it, shield it.

But *who* from? And *why*?

No! This posture was an instant giveaway, it only revealed more fully and in full glare, what she wanted to conceal.

"What a futile attempt at masking one's vulnerability! It only highlighted it, exaggerated it, aggravated it even!"

She knew it too well. And not for a second did she believe that others would buy a story that she herself had no conviction in.

Drawers were being pulled frantically, pans were banging against each other, jostling for space, trying their best to fit in perfectly with their neighbors. Taps were being opened, closed, and opened to allow some water to trickle down, only to be closed again. There was, however, no sequence, no clarity in what she was doing. She didn't know how to prioritize her "to-do" list.

What came before what? What was most important? What demanded her attention first and foremost?

All she felt was a deep, boring, burning sense of urgency consuming her, drilling constantly, cruelly in her cranium and spreading, expanding like a shadow, creeping stealthily along the nape of her neck. Damn those temporal arteries that danced violently! If only one could firmly affix girdles there and contain those pulsations. One strong punch and boom! No more of that tormenting, thunderclap, recalcitrant ache. Oh! One could rein it in, for sure. All demons could be conquered, sooner or later. Yes, it was painful, yes, she was wringing her hands repeatedly, yes, she was stomping her feet forcefully, yes, the white of her eyeballs seemed to be popping out of their sockets, but it was all going to be alright. One just had to learn the trick. It would come, it would surely come. In this lifetime, it would...

Until then, one patiently needed to keep rubbing the floor...

And hold onto the music of the orange wind chimes playing softly in the gentle breeze that blew inside her heart....

Dear Sun,

Today as I was buying some fruits from the woman that puts up her cart near our apartment, she taught me an important lesson. That of honesty. Here's how...

"Aunty, can I please have four bananas and two oranges?" I asked her.

She replied, "Take five bananas instead. For twenty, you can take five. How can I cheat you? How can I be dishonest? If I do, would it not come back to me in a terrible form? Won't my body, my legs, my arms give up on me, then? Won't I fall face down?"

Today, she was my teacher, Sun.

It made me look up for this. You might agree with me here H. Your Iqbal spoke thus,

Koi Qabil Ho Tau Hum Shan-e-Kai Dete Hain
Dhoondne Walon Ko Dunya Bhi Naee Dete Hain!

On him whom merits well, I set the brightest diadem,
And for those who truly seek, a new world awaits!

Not only did this lady give me an extra banana that I neither asked for, nor expected, but, in fact, she taught me something very important. Again, a lesson, I thought I didn't need. But see, He is bent upon teaching me just what I thought I didn't feel the need for. You get my drift? Forty rupees for such pearls of wisdom! I wish to etch them forever in my heart, imbibe them, embody them, hence I write it all to you. And in the process, reiterate it to my own self.

Yesterday, as he wanted to buy himself a new pair of glasses, I followed suit. He tried one after another after another. He was merely checking them out, he didn't really want to buy. Neither did he have to. But as he was trying them on, I learnt something else. It's not just the glasses that we needed to change, but our eyes and our vision. It tends to become so skewed, so narrow, so constricting. What can one see with any degree of clarity when your eyes are befogged and cloudy? Absolutely nothing, wouldn't you agree? But then again, thankfully, even when there is no sight, there is an insight into what is missing. So, whose eyes are they then, you think? Mine or His? When I close my eyes, He opens His. When I sleep, He awakens. What should be my endeavor, then? To synchronize my awakenings with His. To redirect, realign. Gently, softly, naturally. I don't have to do it. I just have to not resist when He chooses to awaken in me and not refuse the path set out for me to walk upon. Even in His absence in me, lies the shadow of His presence. The awareness of that niche, the space left vacant inside me where He ought to be, is an ode to Him. Let's call it 'ishq e ghaibana'... Love in absentia, shall we? You do understand the pang of separation I feel here, don't you?

So, when I returned, I did not prostrate before Him. But I felt each cell of my body bending its head in His direction. Something tells me, He accepted my humble unvoiced gratitude.

Kal meri benamazi mei bhi namaz thi

Yun to meri namaz mei bhi benamazi hoti he

With love,

S.

She set out once again

in the dimness of the night

to walk the path of faded memories

to feel that soft touch of snow

beneath her frozen feet...

Icicles were formed,

she had heard today

those crooked, sharp daggers

formed but from her tears

lay frozen, on the sloping roof of her heart

suspended, imprisoning,

what was to freely flow

All seasons froze too

in that one dying breath

Beneath that layer of white

those auburn autumn leaves

that first blossom of spring

183

And her heart was laid bare

crushed and smothered

She paid no heed

plain foolish indeed!

She moaned, she wailed

in that freezing cold

as heartlessly, her stories were sold

her pain, the agony

the refusal to live

Frozen, she lay

until that morning came

when all icicles would melt....

"Some of the most timeless and achingly beautiful love stories are those that spoke of unrequited love," she was told.

It had made her mouth curl up in a smile. No, she didn't find it amusing, the smile wasn't sardonic in the least bit. She was too young, too foolishly naive then. She was no expert on love, no expert on stories either, romantic or otherwise. Not *then*, not *now*. Yet, she had felt a strange nudge on her heart. Someone had managed to pull those loose strings, and pull them fiercely, *savagely* even. She had wanted to believe every word of it, she had wanted to believe it so badly. The impossibility of love made the possibility of creating martyrs out of everyone, a reality. It was a high as no other drug could ever possibly provide. It must have captivated the hearts and minds of so many before her. And each must have felt so special, so *singularly unique* in his or her experience of it, that it was surprising one never felt the need of patenting the exclusivity of one's ascension in this fall.

Yes, we all wanted to 'fall' in love. Fall and how!

We wanted to be soldiers that never saw the light of the battlefield. We were all rebels, we raised our obstinate heads in mutiny, yet none of us wanted to go through the pain of biting the bullet. In this game of succession, we wanted to be the natural heir to the throne, undisputed, uncontested. We wanted to smell the sweet fragrance of this rose, crush those bloody petals and make a tiny bottle of perfume (*Gulab attar*, perhaps?) for our sake, yet we were unprepared to be pricked by the thorns that accompanied the process. And no, we didn't want to have anything to do with watering this plant constantly either. We had no time for that nonsense! We were too busy with far more pressing matters. We were all warriors here, each one of us, revolutionaries in this struggle to give up one's freedom and give it up wholly, willfully. *Gladly.*

There was some truth in it, after all. In the song that would play in her room so often. She could solve complex problems in physics to that rhythm once. It now seemed like an eternity ago...

'Wise men say only fools rush in, for I can't help falling in love with you...'

How often had she heard Elvis serenade her in his baritone voice? This impossibility of love made everyone's heart swoon with desire, it made us devious, devilish and delirious. We could proudly claim to be *'romantics'* in our own right. War veterans we all wanted to be, those wounded by the sharp rapier of unfulfilled love and we could then proudly brandish our self-imposed scars like shiny medallions on our swollen chests and even more inflated egos. Our feet would barely touch the ground beneath us, we would float instead. Levitate! Glide and soar!

There we were, right up there! Perched precariously on cloud nine! We wanted to reach the pinnacle and remain there, perennially, permanently. No, we didn't have the patience to climb up the steep ladder, painfully slowly, one step at a time. When the doors of reason were closed, we wanted to jump right into the vast emerald waters of the ocean of impossible, unreasonable love

Hazrat Shah Niyaz' unreasonable plea to reason seemed so apt...

'Aql ke madrasse se uth, ishq ke mai kadey mei aa'...

Abandon the school of reason, come! Lose yourself in a tavern of inebriating love....

Hum kya chahte? Azadi!

This war cry kept reverberating in her demented head.

She had inherited this ailment as a part of a yet unrecognized, undiagnosed disease that had afflicted not just her, but an entire breed of people, that wanted love *minus* the responsibility of loving, that wanted the fast food of love to be served steaming hot on a platter, with a sprinkle of French fries by the side, if you please. And we could junk it up further, by adding a whole can of fizzy drink while the fizz hadn't yet fizzled out. We could

186

hog on this sumptuous feast like greedy gluttons, burp loudly and forget all about it. No, one needn't feel guilty, for we could poke our fingers in after each binge, retch and vomit all that love out in one go. Yes, we were love-bulimics.

Love for home…Love for freedom…Love for self…

What was love? Loving what you desired, *how* you desired and *when* you desired? She wondered.

What was love?

Chasing the unattainable? Yearning, pining and longing for what we didn't have and *couldn't* get? Was love a conquest? A triumphant war cry bellowed to drown our inner voids? A cerebral *Kamasutra?* Mental gymnastics? A wicked tickle to be felt on the supposedly deep sulci of our primitive brains? Or a gray area titillating the convolutions of our gray matter?

A dream? A vision? Or a reality?

What was *real* love, *really*! Humbug!

Real love was hard work, he was teaching her today. It required immense patience, patience to change oneself and the other, both. Real love required several deaths and we were all so petrified of dying. Yes, martyrdom was all very good, it was desirable even, for it allured us with the lip smacking promise of Paradise. It made us assume an air of nobility. We all wanted to reach the highest seat of Heaven, but were we ready to die?

"Jaam e fana o bekhudi ab to piya jo ho so ho"…

Drunk on this wine of self-annihilation,

this unawareness of self, I lay intoxicated,

whatever befalls my heart,

I shall now embrace with my all...

Steadfast I remain, come what may...

Love told her to keep dying yet feel vibrantly alive in each death. His heaving chest, his snores were music to her ears. It was so comforting--her home away from home.

Tonight, *this* was love. His snores were an anthology on love.

And this love was *returned, reciprocated, requited*. The *real* reward lay in *loving,* not in *merely* being loved. This tree would see all seasons, the leaves would fall in the fall and new flowers would spring up each spring. It was tender, bitter-sweet and had an obnoxiously pungent odor on days.

Love was real...

Wasn't this achingly beautiful too?

She smiled in the dark as tiny fireflies lit up her heart in a warm, radiant glow.

Chapter 5

The search for love

There was love and then there was that vague shadow of it.

There was love--obvious, apparent, in the everyday, the mundane and then there was that sketchy, hazy, obscure idea of it. Where was love for her? On what peaks? In what depths? In which 'home'? In the 'heart' of which lover? Was it in the mother's belly, where we floated in our own urine, drowned in our own stench, eyes closed tightly, hands clutching our tiny hearts, where we drank that very first nectar of life, that coming out of us, going back into our bodies? Or was it in that sudden spurt of blood that gushed forth before the umbilical cord was clamped down and cut? Why couldn't she see it today? Smell it, touch it or hear it? Even *that* love changed forms, as did everything. There were no constants in the shifting frames of life, one picture gave way to another, one wave blended with the other and that's how the entire ocean took turns in reaching the shores, barely touching it, receding even before it had tasted its own saltiness against the wet grains of the rust sand.

Was there love in staying on even as it tormented one's heart, or was it in running away as fast as one's feet and cowardice could take? Did it beat fiercely in that wild thumping of the wounded heart caught in the middle of a raging, tumultuous sea or was it shed as tears of anger and anguish in moments of utmost despair? Was it exhaled out in the erratic, shallow, uneven breathing of a troubled existence or gasped hungrily back in a frantic bid at survival?

Even as the cutting edge of her pain met the acute sharpness of his, she knew at once. This was not love, not yet. Neither was that other skeleton any closer to it, that nebulous, ambiguous, intangible, incomprehensible, vague notion--the idea that existed in her head, in abstruse books, in poignant songs. The *idea of love*, seemed revolutionary no doubt, and just like every other idea, it had been captivating, exhilarating even! That romantic notion of 'home' desired by the homeless. That idea of freedom for the incarcerated! It had held immense promise. In fact, it had seemed thrilling, dizzyingly exciting, intoxicating and inebriating, even! But can such ideas see the light of day? Could it have survived the darkness of the darkest of nights? She had seen enough of 'love' to know the answer to that one. No, love demanded much more. So much more than mere ownership, much more than the ego would allow or make concessions for. Love was not merely in living, but in dying, too. And these deaths were exacting, for they touched not just ones' exterior, they killed something deeper within, and occurred not once, but several times. Ghalib says it so painfully...

"*Humein kya bura that marna, agar ek baar hota*"....

Who would detest death, if only it were to occur just once?

Yet, living outweighed death. It was far more heroic an act than dying, and living *while* you were dying from within, was an indescribable feat, an unmatched triumph, an unparalleled tour de force, where life, death and love went hand in hand. Did these young boys in Kashmir dream of freedom just as she dreamt of love? The same hope? The same mad fervor?

Unconditional love! She laughed at the mere sound of it! This was the biggest lie that we had foolishly created to help us go through the banality of everyday life. It was an escape as was 'romanticized' love. A blatant lie, a hypnotic. 'Real' love, when one *did* reach that station in life, was terribly difficult. It was a war waged against oneself, against one's idea of oneself, against the very core of one's being, against each fiber of one's inner robe. And not once, but every single day, in moments of awareness and oblivion both, in the consciousness of knowing, in the unconscious state of not knowing and in the powerful, pervasive subconscious too. All this was so tough! So tough! He was ripping her very soul apart, shredding it to smithereens.

She was hungry, she needed food for her soul. She gobbled down the minced meat he had made painstakingly for her. "Isn't this good enough for me?" she wondered. It filled her belly, yes, but she needed to learn to help it satiate her soul's desires as well. It required training. It was traumatic, she could see that. Her deciduous teeth had to be shed, and permanent ones had to break through the soft, raw, inflamed gums. She had to keep pulling at the ones that hung only so lightly, as if by a flimsy piece of invisible tissue. But this *last* pull was agonizingly painful. And she was savoring it insanely. Then again, there was no other road to salvation, no other path that would lead one inside.

So much for love! Her mind admonished her. Enough of this musing!

Love... Love... Love...

She was snapped out of her reverie irreverently, by the beep of the washing machine.

Where was this love each time she loaded the washing machine with a bunch of dirty clothes, stained and smeared with the struggles of living? All that muck, grease and grime would be removed, each time those clothes were spun and tumbled mercilessly, the sleeve of his shirt, hopelessly entangled with the hem of her skirt. Each such wash washed away all faded notions of love. Yet each such wash purified it, cleansed it

191

and made it new, untainted and pristine. Each such wash colored the other's garments, unmistakably, unavoidably, her reds staining his whites, her blues coloring his greens. Even when no color was obvious to the eye, one could *simply* tell where her clothes had clung onto his, and where his hand had clasped hers, as both were being impossibly wrung and twisted in all possible directions, spun round and around in circles. Each eddy created a menacing tempest, a formidable hurricane that posed a threat to both their individual and collective existences. To be washed *thus,* with the other, to be cleansed and stained at the same time, was such an exhausting ordeal. And it had to be repeated each day, without fail, whether their clothes were filthy or clean. This ritual *just had* to be followed. Did it matter then, whether we prostrated before the Unseen when we were bending our heads for the raiment chosen for us? And in the process, changing our bodies and souls too, to fit into those clothes, expanding and shrinking alternately? Bowing in the direction of the sun's rays, we were bright yellow sunflowers that were reaching out for some light.

"Was *that* love?" she asked herself.

They didn't know how they reached out for each other. They were lying on the bed like old, battered comrades, defeated and strained beyond measure, exhausted *and* in exile. He was reading out a book to her, upon her repeated insistence, for she was too tired to read it herself. In fact, she seemed too tired to do anything herself, these days. Her nuchal muscles were buckling under the tremendous weight of the world she had been carrying upon her shoulders. No! There was very little air in the room, she remarked. She needed to go out. And so, she jumped out of the bed. She was nearly gasping for air, well, *mentally*, at least! And he gave in to her vicissitudes without much protest, like he always did. This was one quality she *absolutely* loved in him, the way he indulged her, even when she knew she was being obnoxiously unreasonable.

She wanted to be taken somewhere, *anywhere*. Somewhere she could breathe freely. Where her own mind didn't put her in a tizzy, where nothing mattered, not him, not her, nor the constraints of time. She wanted to tread softly under the glinting gaze of the moonlight, her nimble steps gliding over a thicket of grass. She wanted to feel each tiny blade tickle her feet, playfully, impishly, she wanted to walk amidst the twinkling stars, drift past the clouds, she wanted to be rowed gently across the *Dal* Lake, *towards* the shore, but never really *reaching* it. She wanted to gaze at the moon in broad daylight. Could she stroll blithely upon a carpet of her own dreams? Could she roll over and over in the silken softness of those virginal hopes? They could silently watch the sun's rays filter in, through the lacy network of interwoven breaths, warming their hearts, putting it on fire perhaps? Oh! She could go on and on... And on...

They decided to go to a park finally. The very thought of sitting on the green grass eased her pain, albeit temporarily. Distractions were a welcome relief. What was life anyway, other than a series of distractions that we tended to create? But before she could throw on her clothes, she found herself being drawn in, slowly into his arms. She let herself melt. She was done resisting life, done refusing love. When life calls, when love beckons, you don't fight, you don't kick your heels and run away at a galloping pace. Instead, you hold your ground, you let life plant a tender kiss on your withered lips, gently, gingerly; you let the breath of life aerate your lungs and your being.

New lovers are like children thrown abruptly into the sea. They don't know how to swim, but they instinctively know how *not* to drown. They are like explorers--bold, daring, inquisitive and thirsty. They navigate through each other's bodies timidly at first, testing waters, until they slowly unearth the treasure trove hidden beneath each other's layers of skin, naturally finding the right pace, neither too fast, nor too slow, *just* the right mix, one that matches the beating of wild hearts, hearts racing in unison, synchronized with each shallow breath, dancing with it, swaying, matching step for step.

Guided by no more than intuition, they dive into each other's bodies, in one huge leap of faith, leaving their own carapaces behind, cast away carelessly, hurriedly as the clothes they shed feverishly--one becoming the other, discovering the pleasure of the other, the opposite, the contrast-- the brilliance of light accentuated by absolute darkness, they melt, they blend,

193

they dissolve, immiscible elements seeking merger. *Water and fire. Fire and water.* In each other's arms. Water quenching the thirst of the raging, lapping tongues of fire, and fire making the tepid water crackle and boil over. Each touch, each kiss, each rub on the skin was an intermingling of contrasts. Water dousing fire and fire making water scald and sear. This sultry, sensuous dance, this hide-and-seek, made hearts soar. Love was a pill that made one forget. It aided amnesia, she thought later. Immersed so fully in the other, aware of one's own body, yet oblivious of one's nakedness, one simply could not remember anything that came before or that *was* to come. It was just *now*, all that mattered was *now*, this breath, this sigh. As eyes closed gently, hearts and souls opened, one leading to the other.

As she was gently laid on her back, she muttered under her breath.... *Become the death I need....* Lovers killed each other and, in this death, lay the hope of birth, rebirth, a new cycle. No, love did not take you on another plane, it wasn't *supposed* to. Not for her, at least. Not anymore. Love only anchored you firmly in the present, in the *here,* in the *now*. There was unity in this trinity--of mind, soul and of body. It was no magic, no music, yet there was an unmistakable rhythm to it that no ear could miss, no eyes could be blind to. The first knock, that first move, that first opening was always difficult. That is how Nature worked, for nothing of any consequence could ever be born without a painful death. And to admit another inside you, to open your legs and heart and soul to another, required not one but several deaths. This flower had to be plucked, snapped away from the tree that bore it, for only when it was extricated thus, could it blossom and bloom more fully.

How petrified is a suckling of losing her nest, her sanctuary, her 'home!' If only she knew of the vast azure skies that await her on the tilted side of this fear. Perhaps it would then, not be this afraid of letting go, of leaving the warmth of her nest and joining the other in building a new one, twig by twig. But to open the slammed doors of your own being to the other, to admit the other into your soul was painful. Painful, but necessary. It had an acutely profound meaning, it was symbolic. To her, it signified, a breaking of all barriers that had barricaded her heart, of becoming fluid, permeable, transparent, flowing. Continuous waves would then, originate from the underbelly of her ocean and strike the other's shore, each ebb, followed by a flow. The gentle rocking of the waves, the to and fro oscillations of the pendulum, the clutching, stiffening fingers and the sudden, rapid releases, the deafening silences, the soft murmurs and the animal yelps all rose and fell in lyrical succession. As she gripped his dimpled, white shoulder, she knew that the terrain of her heart would never be the same again. The arid deserts of her heart had soaked in the water of these unexpected rains, and now pliant and soft, she had engraved his dimple on it. In this delicate deflowering, new seeds were being sown in the soil hidden beneath their bosoms.

It was the first time that she walked alone on these streets in Delhi, where she had been living for the past many months. Living and yet not living. She had been xenophobic. The city was strange, and she didn't take to strangers too warmly. The city had reciprocated in the same vein, not opening to her either. She had yearned for the skies of familiarity, for the snow-clad mountains, for joyous *shikara* rides, pined for the clock to rewind for her sake, for the sake of good old times. She had wanted old friendships to be renewed, wanted to reverse life, relive her childhood, even. "I hadn't done it right then," she thought. She would fix the loopholes if given a chance; she would do right all that now seemed terribly wrong. She was just romanticizing the past and so was filled with regret. Didn't we all feel this way at some point or the other? She thought.

"He doesn't want to accept that the Kashmir of his childhood exists no more, that it no longer *is*. It's gone, vanished, moved on, changed, mutated…Kaboom!"

This is what her aunt had once told her, talking about her uncle's persistent longing for things to be 'like before.' She remembered exactly where they were, in the backyard of their house in Kashmir, standing next to the green wooden frame of the crisscrossed barrier that separated their annex from their main house. On her right, was a hand pump which was used to water the vegetables that her grandmother had sown in a part of their garden, ear marking that territory as hers. We were strange animals.

"We, like dogs, mark our territories," he had once told her.

Oh yes! We were strange and how!

We attached and then, found it emotionally traumatic to detach. We couldn't even detach from the ghost of our own long-lost memories easily, we kept clinging to the past as a child would cling onto his parents' legs, crying not to be pushed inside the classroom. And here, she was holding onto entirely different things, refusing to be pushed into this school of life. Who knew what teachers she might find? Who knew what lessons she would have to unlearn? Learning new things as an add-on seemed easier, but unlearning was so tough.

And here, today, as she was walking on those streets of Delhi alone for the first time, she spotted, in front of a temple, a couple of stalls that sold flowers. She had a sudden, inexplicable urge to buy a rose. Just *one* rose. She smelled the bunch that looked freshly sprinkled with water, the red petals glistening in the fading sun. They bore no smell. They were long stemmed, looked pretty, but had no fragrance whatsoever.

"How bland!" she thought to herself.

"I want a rose that smells sweet", she asked the flower seller. He fished in a white box made of thermocol and took out a tiny red one, that had an even tinier stem, but it smelled divine. "Here, the *desi* rose, one that is grown locally," he said handing the red rose to her. "Don't you have one that has a long stem and still smells sweet? One that could be put in a vase and emanate fragrance all around?" she asked. "No, you couldn't get both," he said. You had to choose, it was an either/or situation. She chose fragrance. She took that rose and enclosed it in her fist delicately and walked towards the park where she was to join him. Once there, she put it in her hair.

It's been a week since she bought that rose. It began withering the very same night. She put it randomly in a book that rested on her bedside table.

And here's where that rose found its resting place... In the company of this poem...

What you have despised in yourself

They are here with us now,

those who saddle a new unbroken colt

every morning and ride the seven levels of sky,

who lay down at night

with the sun and moon for pillows.

Each of these fish has a Jonah inside.

They sweeten the bitter sea.

They shape-shift the mountains,

but with their actions neither bless nor curse.

They are more obvious,

and yet more secret than that.

Mix grains from the ground they walk

with stream water. Put that salve

on your eyes and you will see

what you have despised in yourself

as a thorn opens into a rose

Rumi

She brought that wilted, withered rose near her eyes, letting it touch her closed lids. Its redness had now deepened to a rich crimson with a slight tinge of black. It had withered, yes. But it had somehow acquired a smooth, velvety texture too. In its dryness, in its thirst for water, it seemed to have learnt to moisten its lips with its own nectar and now glowed in its own sheen.

And the fragrance remained, locked forever in its shriveled-up petals, and trapped in the rose of the poem...

In the twilight of unseen dreams

I lay motionless and still

with half closed eyes,

and a half-closed heart

I ripped the darkness of the skies

hoping for the distant stars to gleam.

I groped, I grappled, I grabbed and fumbled

It slipped through the cracks of my unsteady fist

With half closed eyes

and a half-closed heart

only the dark shadow of dreams could be seen

I unclasped my hands

unlocked my heart

opened my eyes to see

And what do I find?

The lock was mine

so, must I be the tumbler and the key

With an unfettered heart

and an unclogged eye

through the darkness of the sky, I begin to see

those tiny twinkling stars now winking back at me....

Epilogue

They had come a long way, her and him. Both literally and figuratively. They had walked slowly at first, then jumped right in, stumbled at every bend, scratched their knees and bruised their hearts, bumped their heads against impassable dead ends, stood immobile, frozen, paralyzed, then rushed at dizzying speed, until they finally found themselves sitting on a bench under the starry sky. How many things had she thrown *at* him, *towards* him, *away* from him. There had been phones flying across parks (highly symbolic, after all, they had started this journey with one phone screen breaking and here they were about to end this chapter with another one in shambles), dinner plates were flung, hands were bitten, stomachs were punched and yes, she had dazzled herself with a spectacular kick that would make any Kung Fu champion run for cover! Bruce Lee would have been proud of her (her brother had practiced all those moves on her)! From door slamming to howling, from slapping to getting slapped, from throwing tantrums to finally throwing in the towel, yes, they were fatigued beyond measure. She had exhausted all her resources of finding faults with him and finding faults in her life--there were either too many to count or there were absolutely none! In any case, she had decided to leave this arithmetic to someone else up there, where the stars blinked tremulously, while they blinked their tired, sleepy eyes down here.

They sat under the black canopy of a beautiful spring night, studying the stars in silence--the ones that twinkled were stars, she was told, while the ones that didn't, were satellites. She wanted to believe this without even blinking her eyes, without even batting her eyelids. She chose not to check the veracity of this claim. She wanted to let their stars *be* now, whether they twinkled or not, whether they blinked or not. For her, they were no more than little lanterns of prayers blown into the air, rising up, *high up* to illuminate their dark nights, they were the almonds she had sprinkled on a cake that she baked for him today, they were the dust of her words that had waxed and waned, withered and blossomed, stretched their arms and curled up and now shone through the blackness of the night, they were her silver tears captured permanently in an everlasting smile, a smile that sparkled *through* the tears, a smile *awash* with tears, a smile *irrigated* by tears.

Love was not a postcard picture, a moment of perfection captured at the right time. Love was imperfect, it was flawed. *Terribly flawed.* So was life. And its beauty lay in its flaws. It was sensuous poetry in motion, the clunking noise of pans striking against each other, it was stillness and the cold sighs that broke that silence. Love was a constant 'work--in--progress.' It was a pilgrimage, a journey, not a predetermined destination. Love was what remained underneath the rubble of a massive earthquake, when all weak structures were razed to the ground, it was that faint shadow of permanence in a largely ephemeral space. Love was the fire on one's neck and the dryness of one's cracked lips too, it was the thrill of wildly pulsating, dancing carotids. Love was a bent back and the sound of one's own heart heard through the diaphragm of a stethoscope, it was a burnt overcooked chicken served with care, it was both white Amsterdam flowers arranged neatly in a vase and a seed sown in the dreary deserts. It had the sharpness of a bee's sting and the sweetness of honey. It wasn't a flash of lightning, nor the deafening thunder, but the silent, rejuvenating rains that percolated the earth and raised the level of its water table from underneath, even when the surface seemed hopelessly dry. It was a well that was hidden somewhere in the heart of the desert, a well that would be found when ones' thirst overshadowed everything else. Love was buying onions together, weighing them, bargaining for them. It was a kind hug given in vulnerable moments and an understanding of those fragile moments.

Love was simply *being*.

Yes, love was *being* there, even when one wanted to simply run away. It was like gardening, for it required a painstaking tilling of the soil of one's soul, letting it stay dormant, unused, unsown too, watering it incessantly, finally sowing tiny seeds, and then waiting patiently for the seeds to sprout. The huge tree that loomed large over their balcony in Delhi, their first balcony together, had acquired grape like bunches that burst into orange flowers. Love was the dehiscence that caused those seeds to burst open their hearts and reveal the fragrant rose hidden underneath, it was finding the Divine in the ordinary, in the banal. It was training one's soul constantly to be open, it was the brightness seen on gloomy days and the imperceptible rustling of leaves in a gentle breeze. Love was a collective serendipitous discovery of the sharpness of Kashmiri garlic in Delhi, a knowledge shared by a stranger in hushed tones, it was defrosting the cold refrigerator of one's heart, twice every week and mopping the wet floor if the water overflew. It was no epiphany, no bolt out of the blue, no smooth ride, no perpetual stumbling block. It was a repetitive derailing of one's soul and then pulling one's socks to clean up all the mess, putting this train back on track-- a track that would lead to unknown places.

Love was in the monotony of knowing and in the excitement of not knowing. It was in embracing a contrast. It lay in the comfort of the slanting roofs of one's homes left behind and the open terraces of roofless homes too. Love was in hugging misshapen bodies and seeing beauty in bleary, blotchy, sleep deprived eyes. It was way beyond form, far deeper than that. It spoke clearly and resoundingly in shared silences....in the comfort of finding *home* in each other and in *oneself,* when the geography outside shifted abruptly as tectonic plates collided with each other throwing up new, jagged peaks. Love was in scaling those peaks, carrying all your parts within, in harmony, in a gentle, tender equilibrium. It was the process of learning patience, with oneself and the other.

Love was taming the unruly in oneself, finding a more tempered, a more nuanced expression of self. It was learning a new language, creating a new narrative, writing a new story.

It was fire juxtaposed with water, it was kissing one's Achilles heel, repeatedly.

Love was finding something new in the same old drudgery.

It was a song that grew slowly on you...

It was both attachment and detachment taught in one go.

Love was both remembering and forgetting.

An excavation of self, an expedition undertaken inside one's soul.

Love was in both holding on and in letting go...

It was in folding clothes, packing bags and then unpacking, unfolding them all over again.

She was told all this by the little stars that blinked in the dark night...One must *always* believe the stars to be true to their words, for these stars had guided many travelers in these journeys. The stars never lie, they always lead one to the path set out especially for them.

One only had to believe, the stars would speak to us.

One only had to listen....and listen with one's heart.

As the Last Leaf Lands....

Dear Sun

Sitting in a plane all by myself, staring out of the window, I try to ask myself why is it that I'm doing what I am doing. I want to fly. That's all I can think of, now. Yes, I want to fly. Emotionally. Mentally. And thus, I fly in the physical 'plane,' hoping for a strong and resounding message to reach my inner terrain. I see the cottony white clouds floating by, touched gently by the sun's rays, a playful brightening of the brightest of my dreams. I smile despite myself. I sprinkle the sparkling stardust of my smile in the deep gorges below. The same gorges that had become my 'vale of wail.' I sigh no more, I smile instead. I let my laughter echo in the mountains, my jaw widening as I see the sculpted jagged peaks.

Nimble feet, I stand atop the precipice, lunge my entire body forward and wait for the precipitous fall! Thud! I feel the blast of air on my skin, propelling me forward, as I widen my arms to embrace the cold wind, each tiny molecule, each minute particle. From now on, I am my own parachute. I am my only root. I am the only thread that connects these dotted lines, that silken soft golden thread that runs through the centre of my tree's spine. The leaves that were shed were also mine. And so, shall be those curled tendrils that would raise their tiny, tender heads. I am the music of my pauses and the silence in my conversations. I am spreading my wings,

208

more fully now. We all have in our fates reserved those falls. If the falls are our own to face, why must the heights scaled be decided by others? I want to be the depth of my deepest falls, the cushion, the ground, the sky above. All! I want to be these clouds drifting by, the blue skies, the winds tempered by those gasping sighs. I want to be my own book, the blank empty pages, the golden ink that adorns each letter, the curves, the bends and the tiny dot in the end. I peep down again at the patterned maze. A maze. A gaze. A shift, amaze!

You ask me why I am running away? Why do I keep running away? Today I am not running away, but towards myself. I run towards uncertainty. I run towards fear. I embrace it as I clutch my heart that sinks as the plane descends the mountains and my heart plummets. The plains, the mountains, the plane. I let my heart bounce joyously, up and down and up and down. Look now, it shakes, it vibrates. I let my body be this plane. I shed the garment of fear, for it was all in vain. I know the only truth that lies ahead is life and death, life in death, life after death. I now inhale the mingled breath, the life of breath, the breath of life. I breathe life into death. Don't die each moment, when you can live even in death. Go on, now! This is life. And in its arms is born another death. Celebrate life. Celebrate death. In its folds, in its depth, lay hidden meanings one can never fathom. Scale not these mountains of meaningless words. Shake. Melt. Flow. Flow in the arms of silence....

Put your feet on this ground, step out and tread gently on this land.... Come now... Come, it's time to land....

Fly, you will

Even soar

Some days less

While some, more

But after each flight

Remember

We must land....

We must land....

And with that, she closed her tattered journal with its yellowed leaves and put it away for another day, another summer of blinding insights...

Notes on Sources

1) Khusro, Amir, "Zee hale miskin makun taghaful," *Azkalam,* Web, 2015.
2) Ghalib, Mirza "Ye na thi hamari kismet", *Poemsurdu*, 6 May 2015, Web, 2016.
3) Faraz, Ahmed, "Ranjish hi nahi," *Ajabgjab*, May 23, 2015, Web, 2016.
4) Akhtar, Jan Nisar, "Aayi zanjeer ki jhankaar," The film Razia Sultan, *Youtube*, 6 November 2016, Web, 2016.
5) Ghalib, Mirza, "Har ek baat pe kehte ho tum ki tu kya he," *Poetryone*, 18 September, 2014, Web, 2016.
6) Khusro, Amir, "Khabaram raseed imshab ki nigaar khuahi aamad," *Azkalam*, 25 April, 2012, Web, 2016.
7) Khusro, Amir, "Chaap tilak sab cheeni," *Urdu-sufi-poetry.blogspot*, 11 November 2010, Web, 2016.
8) Surat Al Sharh, 94: 5, The Holy Quran.
9) Faiz, Faiz Ahmed, "Dil na-umeed to nahin nakaam hi to hai," *Ravimagazine*, 2 October 2016, Web, 2016.
10) Iqbal, Allama, "Shikwa Jawab-e-Shikwa," *Amiqbalpoetry*, 2 August 2011, Web, 2016.
11) Niyaz, Hazrat Shah, "Ishq mei tere kohe gham," *Shayri*, 26 September, 2006, Web, 2016.
12) Rumi, "What you have despised in yourself," *Linepainterj.blogspot*, 18 August 2009, Web, 2016.